BLOOD BOUND

A JUNKYARD DRUID URBAN FANTASY SHORT STORY COLLECTION

M.D. MASSEY

MODERN DIGITAL
PUBLISHING

AUTHOR'S NOTE

The events of *Voodoo Ball* occur just before the final chapter of *Druid Vengeance*. If you haven't read that far in the main series yet, beware... spoilers ahead!

VOODOO BALL

In which Colin attempts to escort Maman Brigitte's grand-daughter to a grand ball, resulting in unexpected consequences...

1

————

I pulled into the parking lot at Madame Rousseau's Palm and Tarot Readings a few minutes after eight in the evening, as requested. Actually I was a few minutes early, because I didn't want to take any chances on being late. After all, this date was payment in kind for a favor from a voodoo goddess... one who also belonged to the Celtic pantheon.

Don't screw this up, Colin.

Despite my nervousness, I thought I was winning in the "good date" department so far. Rather than picking Janice up in the Druidmobile—my vintage Gremlin—I'd instead borrowed a late-model Caddy from the resale lot at the junkyard. I'd even paid one of the guys in the shop to detail it for me, and I was wearing a matching pair of slacks and dinner jacket as well. Hell, I'd even foregone my customary black combat boots in favor of a pair of honest-to-goodness Italian dress shoes.

No tie, though—can't look like I'm trying too hard.

Janice's shop was closed for the evening, so I walked around back to her private residence. Her business was located in a rather nice limestone two-story that was conveniently located right along IH-35. After local residential zoning restrictions had been lifted, the home had been converted into a palmistry and tarot reading shop, with living quarters in the back and on the second floor. It was the perfect place for Janice—or Madame Rousseau, as she was professionally known—to ply her trade, disseminating half-truths and outright lies to the mundanes, keeping them securely in the dark regarding The World Beneath.

I opened the gate that led to the back entrance, checking the wrought-iron and stone fence for wards before I touched it. Janice had a nice little lawn back here, hidden behind some tall shrubbery and a six-foot limestone privacy partition. Why it wasn't warded was beyond me, but I figured it was probably part of her whole "I'm not a real voodoo priestess" schtick.

Ironically, just as I was contemplating the lack of magical protection on her home, the back door opened of its own accord. I cautiously peeked inside, scanning the small but tidy kitchen beyond with a frown.

"Hello? Anyone here?"

A mild and pleasant woman's voice with an ever-so-slight Yat accent echoed down from the nearby stairwell.

"Be down in a minute! Feel free to grab a cold drink or beer from the fridge if you're thirsty."

With nothing better to do, I walked in and took a seat at the kitchen table—a mid-century modern affair done in chrome and plastic laminate, with padded vinyl chairs to match. After waiting patiently for a good fifteen minutes, I pulled out my phone and started clearing out old messages. Twenty minutes after that and halfway through my task, I heard light footsteps on the stairs. Being a gentleman, I stood to greet my date for the evening.

As Janice walked into the room, a low, almost silent whistle escaped my lips. I'd never seen my friend dressed in anything other than t-shirts, jeans, and low-heeled sandals, and she always wore her hair down straight and parted in the middle. If she'd used makeup before I hadn't noticed, and if I'd previously been asked to describe her, I'd have said she was fit and pleasant-looking in a sort of ordinary, girl-next-door kind of way.

But now—geez. She wore a knee-length skater dress in emerald green, with a lace-bordered V-neck that showed off just the slightest bit of cleavage, a feature that hadn't drawn my attention in meetings past. Speaking of things I hadn't noticed, she had just enough makeup covering her cream-colored skin to accentuate her narrow but not overly-long face, high cheekbones, heart-shaped mouth, and pale grey-green eyes.

In addition, her hair had been pinned up and partially braided, with the braids artfully arranged behind her head. This had the effect of showing off her graceful, slender neck, which was adorned by a stunning silver Victorian choker with a rather large emerald set in the center.

My eyes were momentarily drawn to the stone. It had been cut and shaped *en cabochon,* so it looked almost like a giant mood-stone, of the type used in mood rings from the

70s and 80s. Except there was something mystical about this stone, something magical and mysterious. I couldn't define what it might be—not without offending my date by examining her jewelry instead of admiring the effort she'd put into her makeup and attire.

"Wow, Janice. You look amazing."

She blushed, demurring slightly as she did a quick pirouette. "You like my dress? Gran always said green was my color."

"She was right. The dress and that choker really set off your eyes."

Janice smiled. "You're sweet, Colin. You know, I..." Her eyes glanced over my shoulder at the clock on her kitchen wall. "Crap, we're going to be late!"

Janice grabbed my hand, yanking me toward the exit. Using not a small amount of semi-supernatural alacrity, I managed to slip around her in time to open the door. She passed by me, scurrying along at a decent clip despite the matching emerald-green heels she wore.

"Gah, Gran'll kill me if I miss the formal announcements. How fast is your car?" she asked as she descended her back steps.

I thought about it for a moment. "Very? It's a late-model Caddy, more sports car than luxury vehicle."

Janice stopped and turned, raising one hand to her cheek. "Damn it, I forgot my purse. Can you grab it off the table for me? I don't want to risk breaking a heel walking up those steps again."

"No problem, can do." I ducked back inside, grabbing the small clutch and assuming that since it was the only one on the table, it was the right one. Just as I turned to leave, I heard Janice scream.

I was out the back door and in the yard faster than you could say, "screaming voodoo priestess." When I landed at the bottom of the steps, Janice was sitting on the ground, clutching at her neck and staring at the back wall to her yard. I knelt down beside her, assessing the situation.

"Are you hurt?" She looked at me, stunned. "Janice, are you injured?"

"No, but—that's not supposed to be possible."

"What's not supposed to be possible?" I asked.

"Help me up," she ordered, suddenly all business. I did so, allowing Janice a moment to dust herself off. She scowled, and a dangerous gleam flashed in her eyes. "Gran's necklace, Colin—no one's supposed to be able to touch it but me. And that damned revenant just stole it, right off my neck!"

2

"Wait a minute—that necklace belongs to Maman Brigitte?"

She nodded. "She gave it to me, but really it's just on loan. Colin, we have to get it back."

"What exactly does it do?"

Janice swept her arms in a wide arc around us. "See for yourself. Notice anything different now that the necklace is gone?"

I looked around, shifting my eyesight to observe the magical spectrum. Where before there had been no magical wards or spells protecting Janice's home and business, I now saw it was warded nine ways to Sunday.

"Holy shit, that's a lot of protective magic. The necklace hides it?"

She nodded. "It can be used to either hide the wearer from magic, or to hide magic from others. Gran used it for centuries, back when she split off from the Celtic gods. It kept her relatives from hunting her down when she defected to the Guede."

"I can see how something like that could be dangerous, should it fall into the wrong hands. But wasn't it warded against theft?"

"And against anyone knowing what it is. But apparently, the thief knew what it was after."

Janice paused, leaning on me just long enough to slip off her heels. She spoke a quick spell in French Creole, rubbing a hand along the sole of each foot in turn.

"Sure you don't just want to run upstairs and change? That rev can't have gone far, and I can track one through a rainstorm with my eyes closed. I've... uh... had practice."

"Come on, we're wasting time," she said, ignoring my suggestion as she took off at a sprint. "Gran'll kill me if I lose that thing!"

We ran out Janice's back gate into an alley that was more of a dirt path. She was a lot faster than I might've expected, and I soon found myself losing ground on her, despite being in peak physical condition for a human. Out of curiosity, I assessed the effects of the spell she'd cast on her feet, examining her rather shapely legs in the magical spectrum.

Tricky, tricky. Janice is just full of surprises tonight.

The weaves were refined and efficient, just what I'd expect from someone who'd learned magic directly from a Celtic goddess. Or so I had previously assumed—and seeing her spell work cinched it. Curiously, the casting was a mixture of voodoo and fae magic, a combination of energies that should have been patchwork, but instead appeared to be a rather expert bit of spellcraft.

The spell was not just designed to protect her feet, but it also added a bit of spring to each step she took. It was obviously a take on the seven-league boots legend, and it enabled Janice to move a hell of a lot quicker than me in my human form. I was tempted to stealth-shift, but I could only hold my shifted forms for a short time before needing to rest and recover—maybe an hour partially-shifted and half that when fully-shifted.

Best to keep that trick up my sleeve, for now.

"Janice, slow down a bit, will ya?" I called from the bottom of a fifty-foot hill she'd just bounded halfway up like a jackrabbit on meth.

Janice paused to check my progress over her shoulder. "What's the matter? The mighty druid and god-killer can't keep up with little ol' me?"

"Not without using magic, and if it's all the same, I'd prefer to wait until we know what we're up against before I shift."

Janice sighed in exasperation, hands on her hips. "I know what we're about to face, Colin—I saw the rev with my own eyes. Surely you can handle a wee revenant without resorting to magic."

"Um, not to be a pain," I said as I huffed up the hill, "but I've done a lot of hunting, and my instincts are pretty sharp. In this case, I have a feeling things are not all that they seem."

"Well, yeah," Janice replied. "Obviously this revenant

was sent by a bokor of some kind, someone who knows Gran and wants a bit of her magic. So, when we catch 'em, you can take care of the rev and I'll deal with the pissant who sent it. Deal?"

"Sure, but I still don't want to shift until it's absolutely necessary."

She rolled her eyes and tossed her hair back with a wry grin. "Have it your way, but you're lucky you showed up dressed to the nines tonight. Otherwise I'd leave you behind and deal with this myself."

"Your Gran would end me if I let you do that."

"I know," she said with a sly wink. "So, you'd best not hold things up any longer, or I *will* leave you in my dust. Not to worry, though, I'm fairly certain I know where the rev is going. There's an old pioneer cemetery not far from here, a remnant from the early days of the city. I'm pretty sure we'll find our undead thief there."

I pursed my lips and nodded. "Sounds like a plan. Truth be told, I'm eager to see what else you can do after that fancy spell you cast."

"Oh, I have many talents," Janice purred as she did a quick circuit around me, trailing a finger across my chest. "Stick around 'til later, and maybe I'll show you a few."

Gulp.

"I, uh... that'd be nice."

"You have no idea. Now, keep up!"

The pretty voodoo priestess took off like an Olympic sprinter toward the crest of the hill. I stood there for a moment, both admiring her retreating figure and wondering how Maman Brigitte would react if I slept with her granddaughter.

Colin, what have you gotten yourself into?

3

I hit the top of the hill shortly after Janice, purposely putting on a burst of speed—human speed—in order to catch up with her. In my "only human" form, I couldn't maintain that pace for long, but we didn't have far to go. My date had already slowed her pace, indicating via hand signals that I should use stealth as I jogged to her side.

"The graveyard's just up ahead, and I'm pretty sure the revenant'll be there," Janice said in a quiet voice as she pointed to a line of trees roughly thirty yards distant. "It's an old place, so I doubt that the rev was made there. Nothing but bones in those graves, which means the poor soul was probably killed and turned elsewhere."

"Revenants tend to hunt and hole up in familiar places. If the graveyard isn't the rev's home base, why the hell would it head there?" I whispered.

"Because, likely as not, that's where the damned thing is meeting its master. Now, be quiet so we don't scare it off.

I wanna get that necklace back, and in time to make the ball."

Ah, the ball.

I'd forgotten about it, what with the undead thief and all. Likely as not, my clothes and Janice's dress both were going to get all kinds of messed up if things got hairy. I wondered if she was the type who'd have to change instead of just touching up her makeup, should the need arise. Guess I was about to find out.

"Since there's a voodoo practitioner involved, do you want to take point? Or do you want me to see if I can catch it off-guard and end this without a huge fight?"

Janice rubbed her first and second fingers against her thumb on her right hand, as if she were rubbing a piece of cloth between them. I figured it was a nervous habit, something she did when she was thinking. Or maybe she was prepping a spell. Hell, I didn't know. I could recognize voodoo magic when I saw it, but I had no idea how it worked.

"It would be nice to get this done without messing up my dress," she said after she'd considered my offer. "But if you see someone who looks like a voodoo bokor, hang back and let me handle it."

"What's a voodoo bokor supposed to look like?" I asked, truly curious to know if they all subscribed to a particular dress code, or perhaps frequented the same barber.

"Well, they'll have a lot of dead people around them, and they'll stink of necromancy."

"So, pretty much like any other necromancer. Got it." I

pulled my trusty flaming sword Dyrnwyn from my Crane-skin Bag, willing it to remain extinguished so I didn't give away our position. "Give me ninety seconds before you make your entrance."

"Entrance? What, like I'm going to go in there breathing fire and shooting lightning bolts out my ass?" Janice frowned at me. "I'm hardly that kind of witch, and nothing like my Gran. I prefer a more subtle approach."

"I didn't mean anything by it, I just meant that—"

She brayed quietly in a sort of snorting, honking sound. For a moment, I wondered if she was possessed. Voodoo priestesses were known for that, after all. But no, her noisome seizure was something else entirely.

Is that—is she laughing?

Our previous meetings and discussions had been all business, and thus I hadn't offered her much in the way of humor on those occasions. Janice tried to stifle it so as not to make more noise than necessary, but she sounded like a goose with a cold. Moments later, she was wiping tears from her eyes.

"Oh, Colin. Gran was right. It is easy to get a rise out of you."

"Well, that's one thing you have in common with her—a penchant for making me uncomfortable." I smiled to be a good sport, pointedly avoiding any mention of her zany, off-putting laugh. "Anyway, I'm going to sneak up on the necklace thief now. Remember, ninety seconds."

She gave me a wide-eyed grin that said she thought I was a riot. I heard her snort-chuckling as I slunk off into the trees to our right. As I crept through the little patch of woods surrounding the graveyard, I could just make out the age-pitted, moss-covered gravestones that dotted the clearing. A rusted chain-link fence surrounded the grave-yard, probably put there to keep the local kids out. In all honesty, though, the place was creepy enough that any teen would steer clear of it.

It took maybe a minute to sneak to the other side of the graveyard, and a few seconds more to case the place. It consisted of a small patch of grass and tombstones, maybe a hundred feet across and almost completely overgrown with weeds and brush. Sadly, it appeared none of the graveyard's occupants had descendants who were still around to keep the place up.

Or perhaps none are still alive to see to that task.

Although the place looked to have been abandoned by the living, the occupants themselves were definitely in attendance. I spotted the revenant, a tiny little wisp of a thing that couldn't have been older than twelve when he'd been murdered. That one was surrounded by a dozen or more animated skeletons in various states of disrepair. Most were just bones held together by desiccated strands of sinew, with a few patches of moldy skin and clothing covering them here and there.

As for the boy, he was a sad sight. He had a large, jagged gash bisecting his neck just under his chin. It looked as if someone had snuck up on him and slashed him from ear to ear with a saw blade, or maybe a rusty old knife. Although he was most definitely feral and danger-ous, as all revenants were, his appearance saddened me to my core.

Why does it always have to be kids? And who the hell murders a child, only to turn them into a revenant?

I made a mental note to find out who the kid's maker was so I could have a long, painful talk with them. But all feelings of remorse and pity aside, the kid had Janice's choker in his hands—and we had to get that necklace back. I took a last look around to make sure there were no bokors lurking in the shadows. Then, with a deep, shuddering breath, I headed into the graveyard.

4

Once I entered the graveyard, I kept a low profile, slinking from gravestone to gravestone so as not to be seen. Thankfully the skeletons weren't an issue, as far as detection was concerned. Animated skeletons generally lacked the ability to hear, and they mostly operated by direct commands from their master. So long as they didn't see me, they wouldn't detect my approach.

However, their presence might very well mean that whoever raised them was close by. It was a risk I was willing to take, because the sooner we got that necklace back, the sooner I could finish my date with Janice and fulfill my obligation to Maman Brigitte. Not that Janice was poor company, far from it. But owing any kind of favor to a god—especially one of both Celtic and voudon origins—was never a good thing.

I was nearly on top of them when the rev began sniffing the air in my direction.

Ah, shit—my cologne!

I'd slapped some on as an afterthought while I was getting dressed. Normally I didn't use it, nor did I use any scented soaps or shampoos. It was an old habit from my hunting days, just one more trick to make it harder for enemies to detect me. You could always cover your own scent with animal urine, offal, or dung, but it was damned hard to cover up manmade perfumes unless you resorted to magic.

My lack of prescience regarding the potential activities of the evening was about to give away my presence. The revenant had definitely locked in on my scent, probably looking for a meal. There was no way I was going to surprise him now.

Gah! Should've known I'd be facing the supernatural tonight.

I mean, duh. Take one Colin McCool, add a voodoo priestess, multiply by the fact that this was a formal date, and then factor in a half-Celtic, half-voudon goddess as the X-factor, and what do you get? Mayhem, of course.

The rev was looking my way now.

So much for the element of surprise. Time to light this fuse and see what erupts.

I leapt out from my hiding place, swinging Dyrnwyn in a wide arc at the nearest skeletons. The instant it made contact with the first necromantic creature, the dark magic caused the sword to light up like a blow torch. Three of the skeletons split into two on my first swing, and another two of them fell to my backswing.

"Hello, fellas," I said with aplomb as I sauntered into their midst, the sword hanging almost languidly from my grip. "Somebody forgot to invite me to your undead party thingy, so I invited myself. Hope you don't mind."

The rev leapt backward, landing on a short mausoleum-like structure half-sunken into the ground. It hissed at me, clutching the necklace to its breast. A beat after that, the skeletons reacted to my presence, each lumbering toward me with an awkward, shambling gait. As those numbskulls closed in on me, the rev took off at a run in my date's direction.

"Janice, heads up—one jewel thief headed your way!"

Janice didn't reply, so I had to assume that she was lying in wait and somehow laying a trap for our young, unfortunate friend.

Or, she didn't hear me.

Shit.

I laid about with the flaming sword, wasting the undead bone golems with abandon as I ran after the revenant. Thankfully, animated skeletons were slow and clumsy unless under the direct control of their maker. Their current lack of direction made it a simple task to clear a path, which told me I needn't worry about getting blindsided by magic.

Soon I broke free of skeletons and sprinted after the revenant. I hoped like hell that Janice had heard me, but of the few Irish traits I'd failed to inherit from my forebears, luck was chief among them. I extinguished the sword as I ran, because running full tilt with a sword in your hand was hard enough—even when it wasn't on fire.

Moments later, I had the revenant in my sights. It had stopped at the edge of the cemetery nearest Janice's house, probably because it had detected her presence. The voodoo priestess was nowhere to be seen, so I decided to take the opportunity to end this chase while the rev was distracted.

Without slowing down, I slipped my sword in my Bag and leapt at the rev's back. While I could have chopped it down, I was worried that I might hit the necklace it held with Dyrnwyn. The obvious danger was damaging Janice's magical doodad, and the not-so-obvious danger was that the two magical artifacts could react poorly upon contact. It had been known to happen, and the results might be anything from instant transmogrification or a massive explosion to opening a rift in space and time. It wasn't worth the risk, so I tackled the little dead guy instead.

The moment my feet left the ground, I heard Janice call out from the trees nearby.

"Colin, no!"

Well, that can't be good.

Just as I made contact with the revenant, I realized why he had been standing so very still at the edge of the grave-yard, and why Janice didn't want me tackling him. Tiny, nearly invisible bands of mist-like magic enveloped the creature from head to toe, threads so faint I couldn't see them until I was right on top of them. And dancing along those wispy lines of magic were thousands of itty-bitty sparks of electricity.

Wouldn't you know it, those threads trailed straight back to where Janice hid in the trees. For a split second, I had the opportunity to admire her handiwork. It was a neat little spell. The weaves were designed to disrupt electrical conduction in skeletal muscle tissue without doing damage to the target.

A magic taser. Sweet.

And that's the last thing that went through my mind before I got zapped.

5

W hen I came to, my date stood over me wearing an expression that blurred the lines between worry and amusement. Although her brow was furrowed with concern, she was clearly trying very hard not to crack a grin. Meanwhile every muscle in my body ached, likely from the violent spasms induced by Janice's spell. My head felt muzzy, my vision was blurry, and I had a splitting headache coming on.

So, situation normal—all fucked up.

When I'd stopped seeing double, a quick look around the area told me that the revenant was gone. Janice crossed her arms over her chest as she tapped her foot nervously. I could tell she was pissed at me, and the best I could do was apologize for the error.

"Sorry for screwing up your spell. I take it the rev split when you released it?"

She chewed the corner of her lip and nodded. "I couldn't release you without also releasing him, because the spell doesn't work that way. I'd hoped he'd be incapacitated long enough for me to separate you two so I could zap him again. But as I was untangling you, the little turd jumped up, knocked me over, and headed west through the trees."

"Again, my apologies for messing up your trap." I slowly sat up, rubbing my head with one hand while propping myself up with the other. "My compliments on the spell work, though. It packed a punch."

Janice brushed bits of grass and dirt off her dress. "Hadn't ever tried it out on a live person before, or a dead one for that matter, so I honestly didn't know how it'd affect you. Seems the undead recover a lot faster from being zapped by electricity—who knew?"

"Yeah, who'da thunk it?" I replied ruefully. "You said the rev headed west?"

Her expression brightened. "Ah, your memory is coming back. See? You're recovering already. I don't think he's gone far though—"

I cut her off with a wave of my hand. "Janice, what do you mean my memory is coming back?"

"Mmm, well—you were mumbling incoherently for a time, and drooling quite a lot. In fact, you've still got something right there," she said, pointing in the general direction of my face. When my tragically-uncoordinated face wiping attempts failed, Janice hiked her dress slightly to squat down beside me, reaching forward with her thumb to wipe something from my chin. "There you go—all better."

I might've felt like shit, but I still noticed the smooth

curve of her calves—and she noticed me noticing. I blushed a little at being caught, but she merely smiled coquettishly when I noticed her noticing me noticing her.

"Ahem—maybe we should go catch that revenant?" I proffered as I stumbled to my feet.

She stood as well, quicker than me so she could help me up. I almost waved her off, but when my knees began to give, I let her.

Note to self—don't piss Janice off while standing in a mud puddle.

My date cocked her head at me. "Listen, if you're still too weak, I can handle it on my own. That rev's small, and since you took out most of those skeletons, I think I can handle it on my own."

I shook my head. "There were still a few left."

"Nope, took care of them. Pretty easy to de-animate if you know how."

"Still, I should go with you," I said, leaving it unspoken that if I didn't and something happened to Janice, Maman Brigitte would kill me. "Just, ah... give me a moment to fully recuperate."

Closing my eyes, I stilled my mind and slowed my breathing. Then, I changed the rhythm and timing of my breaths, adopting a super-oxygenating pattern that would help clear my head and hopefully allow me to continue the chase. It was an old druid trick, not really magic but instead a learned and practiced manipulation of the human body's capacity to recuperate. In a minute or so, I felt well enough to walk.

"Okay," I said as I opened my eyes. "I'm ready to go."

"Sure, no rush or anything," Janice said, playfully rolling her eyes. "Seriously, though, if you weren't so cute I'd have left your ass in the dirt. So, get a move on already."

She took off at a jog through the trees, but at a much slower pace than earlier. Painfully, I pushed myself to my feet and followed her down a well-used game trail. We ran toward some street lights ahead, passing by an abandoned homeless camp consisting of a collapsed pup tent, a couple of rusted folding chairs, and lots of trash and human refuse.

Secretly, I hoped Janice was right and that we wouldn't have far to go to catch up with the rev again. Although I still felt a bit unsteady, I wasn't going to let her know that. A guy needed to retain some dignity, after all.

Thankfully, my date and I didn't have far to go. We broke from the trees, exiting the small wooded area onto a dead-end street lined with small, rundown single-story homes. Most of the homes had wooden clapboard siding, peeling white paint, and low-peaked, shingled roofs that were about ten years and a few hailstorms past the date they should've been replaced. A few of the houses were brick, and some were brightly-painted in pastel pinks, yellows, and blues. But even the yards that were free of trash and junk displayed the same signs of dilapidation and disrepair you'd find in most poor urban neighborhoods.

Many of the cars parked on the street and in the gravel or cracked concrete driveways were old and in similar disrepair, but here and there I saw late-model luxury cars and SUVs with oversized chrome rims and low-profile tires. The night was still young, and thus some neighborhood residents were sitting on their front porches, chatting, drinking, and listening to music in the mild evening air.

I wondered how the residents would react to a couple of well-dressed white folk chasing a kid up their street. They'd probably assume we were cops and mind their own business, but if there was any gang activity here, we might also draw attention from the wrong people. Just to be safe, I started to stealth-shift. I didn't want to get shot, and it was much easier to take a gun away when you could move at vampire speed.

Now to find that stupid revenant so I can get this date back on track—and pay my debt to Maman Brigitte.

Just as that thought crossed my mind, a scream of sheer terror pierced the night.

"Well, I guess we know where the revenant went," I murmured as I took off at a jog toward the commotion.

6

As we headed toward the screams, I scanned the area while Janice sprinted past me, crouching down behind a rusted 80s-era Pontiac sedan with three flat tires and a cracked windshield. My date peeked over the hood at a house across the street. Her eyes were fixed on the roof of the house, where our errant revenant sat perched in front of an upstairs bedroom window.

The screams, of course, were coming from a teenage girl who stood inside the house just feet from the rev. The thing was covered in blood and gore, and to the untrained eye it likely looked like an extra from a TV zombie show. My first instinct was to cross the street and deal with the rev before it attacked the girl, but her dad beat me to it.

Before I could make my move, a late-middle-aged black man in a wife-beater and tan Dickies work pants appeared in the window, holding an ancient breakover shotgun that looked to be chambered in 10 gauge.

Fucking elephant gun. Gramps knows what's up, apparently.

"Ah, hell no!" the old man shouted. "No triflin' ass white boy's gonna come up on my roof and scare my little girl!"

The old dude stuck the barrel of the shottie out the window and pulled the trigger. The rev screeched like a banshee, then bolted over the eaves of the dormer, stopping at the roof's peak where the old man couldn't see him. The girl's father leaned out the window, shaking his gun at what he must've assumed was a retreating teen.

"Rock salt and ghost pepper flakes! See how you like that, you little bitch-ass punk!" He shook the shotgun one last time before slamming the window closed. "And don't come back!"

Ouch. God love old people who refuse to take anyone's shit. Still need to deal with the rev, though.

I stood up with the intention of taking a running leap at the roof where the rev now crouched, nursing its side. But as I did, Janice motioned frantically at me to stay put.

"Colin, get down!" she whispered.

"What?" I answered, looking up and down the now-empty street.

Rather than drawing a crowd, everyone had gone inside once they heard gunshots. People in poor, working-class neighborhoods knew that you didn't want to get caught outside when the cops came to investigate gunfire. It was just too easy to get implicated in something you had nothing to do with. Best to just mind your own business and be glad it wasn't you who'd gotten shot.

Janice shook her head at me and pointed beyond the house, past the roof where the revenant perched. The rev was just sitting there, moaning and making little gurgly noises while it rocked back and forth to some imaginary beat.

Never seen a rev do that before. Weird.

I watched the unfortunate undead child for a moment, wondering what could be causing it to act so strangely. Then, my eyes tracked beyond the house to the tall trees in the empty lots beyond. It was dark and my enhanced Fomorian eyesight hadn't completely kicked in yet, but I could've sworn that one of the trees was moving.

Even stranger, the trees in this area were mostly live oak and cedar elm. Those species were large trees with lots of foliage that tended to have broad, gnarled trunks. But the tree that was moving was anything but thick and gnarled. Instead, it was tall, slender, and completely devoid of foliage. I kept my eyes on it as I cast a cantrip that would allow me to see better in the low light.

What the fuck?

When it came into focus, I realized that what I'd thought was a tree was no tree at all. Instead, it was a thirty-foot tall man, beanpole thin, wearing battered leather dress shoes, dusty black dress pants, and a matching suit coat with tails that draped down to his thighs. His legs were easily two-thirds his entire height, with arms just as disproportionate that reached well past his knees. He was bare-chested beneath the coat, and so thin as to be almost skeletal in appearance, with ashen skin pulled tight as a drum across his chest, neck, and skull.

His long, thin face looked down on me, and his dark, deep-set eyes fixed on mine.

"'Dis not your concern, druid," he said in a raspy, hollow voice. "Go on den, back to your yard of junk, and leave 'dese matters to 'da loa and Guédé."

At that, the slenderman—because that's what he was, and hell if I was ever going to think of him otherwise—snatched the rev off the roof with one long, thin hand, tucking him into a pocket in his coat. He stepped back into the trees in one smooth motion, displaying a lot more speed and grace than I'd have expected from such an ungainly-looking creature.

"Oh no you don't," I said as I sprinted after the slender giant.

I was past the house and in the backyard when the tall man looked back over his shoulder at me. He sneered slightly, snapping one foot back in a kick that reminded me of someone kicking a dog snapping at their heels. I caught the heel of his massive, size fifty shoe right in the gut. As he followed through, I went sailing across the street, over the houses on the other side and into the yards beyond.

7

————————

I landed on a discarded, rusted washing machine, partially crushing it as it broke my fall. Thankfully, the thing had been scavenged for parts sometime in the distant past, so it was mostly an empty husk that collapsed under my weight. Still, it didn't make for the most pleasant landing. I'd definitely be feeling the after-effects in the morning.

Janice arrived just as I managed to disentangle myself from the remains of the washer. My bumps and bruises had healed already, so I released my stealth-shifted form. If I held it now, it'd be harder to fully shift later. Something told me I was going to need every advantage to beat whatever that thing was that had punted me across the street. Meanwhile my date paced back and forth as she decried this latest development.

"Damn it, Colin—that *files de pute* took off with my necklace. *C'est des conneries!*" she hissed.

I stood, taking a moment to examine and simultaneously lament my shredded dinner jacket and dress shirt. Janice continued to pace and curse, so with nothing better to do I discarded my ruined clothing, replacing it with a warm hoodie that I pulled from my Bag. I kept the slacks and dress shoes, since they were ruined anyway and I didn't have time to change into clothing that would be more appropriate for fighting a thirty-foot-tall slenderman.

After a time, Janice settled down, at least enough to make me think it was safe to approach her. I had no idea how powerful she was, but being the granddaughter of a major loa, I could only assume she could punch above her weight. And I for one did not want to end up on the wrong side of a nasty voodoo curse. Not that Janice had ever indicated she was the type to do such things, but it never hurt to tread carefully around practitioners of witchcraft and other such arts.

"So, you want to tell me about the beanpole?" I asked as I pushed my sleeves to my elbows.

Janice stopped pacing, turning on me with her hands balled in fists. "Who is he? Oh, he's just the second nastiest boogeyman in all of Haitian folklore. And now, he has Gran's necklace. Aw hell, she's gonna kill me for sure!"

I laid a hand on her shoulder. "Now, now, let's calm down a minute and work this through. What's so special about this boogeyman, and why does he pose such a challenge to us in getting that necklace back?"

"Colin, that was Mètminwi, a thing as mean and cross as he is tall."

"Go on..."

"He's not really a loa, although surely he counts himself among them. But he may just be something worse. He's the type of creature that parents invoke to frighten their children when they misbehave. According to legend, Mètminwi roams the night, hunting for people who stay out after dark. And from what I understand, he's particularly fond of children."

I rubbed my chin. "Hmph. What do you think he wants with your necklace?"

Janice wrung her hands as she replied, looking off into the trees. "I don't know—maybe it has something to do with abducting people? He has an agreement with the more powerful loa to only take so many people each night he roams. And he's limited to roaming just once a year. Gran used that necklace to hide from the Tuatha De Danann. You wanna know what kind of evil deeds Mètminwi could hide with it? A lot, that's what."

I exhaled heavily in anticipation of the question I was about to ask. "Janice, what's he do with the people he takes?"

"He eats them, Colin. It's where he gets his power, apparently."

"And the loa put up with that?" I asked. "Seems like Maman Brigitte or one of the other Haitian gods would've put an end to him ages ago."

Janice shook her head. "I don't think you understand the loa at all," she said with a frown.

I rubbed a hand down my face. "Oh-kay. I'll just

assume they're a lot like the fae—dicks one and all. So, tell me what we're up against. What can this Mètminwi do?"

She pressed her palms to her forehead, as if she were massaging away a headache. "Oh, I don't know. He's big, obviously, and somewhat resistant to magic as all the loa are known to be. He has all the powers of a bokor, which is how he raised those skeletons."

"And the rev?" I asked through gritted teeth.

Janice nodded. "And the revenant, which he probably raised just for the purpose of stealing Gran's necklace. Plus he has magic of his own, the kind that allows him to remain hidden, to move from this world to his and back—and to take others with him when he does."

"So, he's your typical evil supernatural entity. You think if we could pin him down, a good ass-kicking would do the trick?"

"He's practically a god, Colin—kicking his ass is going to be a tall order, no pun intended."

"Meh, we'll see about that. Any idea where he went?"

"He took off into the trees and disappeared. And I'd bet bullshit to beignets that he's using Gran's necklace to hide himself from tracking spells." Janice gave the barest shake of her head, her mouth set in a grim frown. "Damn it. I can't help but think we're never going to get it back."

I exhaled heavily, thinking of the poor kid who'd gotten turned into an undead monster just so a minor deity could amass a bit more power. *Fucking dickhead gods.* Necklace or no, Mètminwi was due for a reckoning, and I was determined to see him get it.

"He may not be visible to human eyesight or magic, but a creature his size will leave a trail just the same," I said, forcing a smile. "Cheer up, we'll get your necklace back. Come on, let's get going before he gains too much of a lead on us."

8

J anice stood nearby as I searched the area, crossing and uncrossing her arms as she tried to hide her impatience. Much to my chagrin, Mètminwi had left absolutely no visible sign of his passing. I searched for several minutes using my enhanced sight, but it was as if he'd gone incorporeal. Had he passed into his own realm, beyond our reach?

Then I caught a whiff of something—a musky, piquant odor I hadn't noticed earlier. It was a combination of spiced rum, tobacco, and rotting flesh. I dropped on all fours, getting my nose close to the ground and inhaling deeply so I could mark the scent to memory.

Got you, you son of a bitch.

"Find something?" Janice asked with a note of hope in her voice.

I nodded. "The loa like to drink and smoke, right?"

She arched an eyebrow. "Does Dolly Parton sleep on

her back? They're all practically alcoholics, and smoke like a house fire."

"Then I have his scent. Let's go."

Sniffing along in a crouch like a bloodhound on the hunt, I followed Mètminwi's trail through the small copse of trees, across a few backyards, and into another low-income neighborhood. More than once I lost the scent, forcing us to backtrack so I could pick it up again. A few blocks later, the trail ended at a condemned two-story house on a dead-end street.

The house sat by itself where the asphalt ended, looking out of place next to the small, one-story brick and stucco homes that lined the narrow lane. And the house looked older, too—dilapidated in the way only a home that has been long abandoned can look. White paint peeled from the clapboard siding, the wood beneath had turned gray from exposure to the elements, window glass was nearly non-existent in the panes, and the shutters creaked and banged against the house in the wind. In short, the place was the absolute epitome of a haunted house.

"Why do I get the feeling this house is going to swallow us whole?" Janice asked as we cautiously strolled up the cracked, uneven front walk.

"Maybe because it looks like Nebbercracker's place?" I offered.

"Huh?"

"Never mind," I replied, keeping my eyes on the house. "Look, I doubt this place is simply an empty condemned home. You said Mètminwi can travel back and forth from his world to this one, right?"

"Yep. You think this is the gateway?"

"Mm-hmm, I'd stake my rep on it. Give me a sec—there's no telling where it'll lead, and I don't want to go in there unprepared."

I opened up my Craneskin Bag, rummaging around for my tactical belt. Once I snapped it on, I clipped my holstered Glock 17 to my waistband, along with several spare magazines filled with silver-tipped ammo. Then I slung Dyrnwyn over my shoulder, loosening the sword in the scabbard to ensure I could draw it quickly. Finally, I stuffed my pockets with extra mags that were loaded with iron-tipped and standard ammo... just in case.

Janice observed me as I prepped for battle, a wry grin on her face. "Okay, I have to ask—what's a druid doing with a gun?"

I chuckled. "Long story short? I'm kind of lazy when it comes to learning magic."

"Ah, the 'reluctant druid' thing. I'd heard rumors it had something to do with your ex-girlfriend, but—"

"Can we just focus on getting that necklace back and save the conversation for later?" I snapped, cutting her off before the conversation veered into ex-girlfriend territory.

"Wow. Okay, sorry I mentioned it."

The look of hurt and confusion in her eyes told me I'd been a bit too harsh, and I sighed. "Sorry, but my ex is a sore subject right now, and I really don't care to get into all the reasons why."

She stared at me for a moment with her eyes narrowed, then her shoulders relaxed. "Hey, I get it.

Besides, it's none of my business. I shouldn't have even brought it up."

I didn't know what else to say, so I pretended to be engrossed with checking all my equipment one last time. Janice stood off to the side, hugging herself and staring into the darkness. The silence was unbearable, and she looked like she might catch a chill, so I cleared my throat to get her attention.

"I think I have a windbreaker in my Bag. If you're cold, I mean."

Her brow furrowed as she considered the olive branch I was extending. Finally, her expression softened and she gave a grudging nod. "I'll take it. But don't think this means we're going steady or anything."

I stifled a laugh as I rummaged around in my Bag, handing her the jacket with a crooked grin. "No hard feelings?"

She waved my question away as she pushed the sleeves up on my windbreaker. "Naw. I spent my fair share of time around the Guédé when I was growing up. You gotta have thick skin to hang out with that bunch. Consider it water under the bridge, Colin."

Internally, I sighed with relief. I'd liked Janice before our "date," and I liked her even more after seeing her reactions under stress. Maybe not in a romantic way, but I was decidedly fond of her nonetheless. It wasn't like I had a lot of friends in the World Beneath, not that I could rely on, anyway. I'd hate to think I screwed up a budding friendship just by being a dick.

"Alright, cool." I drew my Glock and racked the slide.

"Now, let's go kick Mètminwi's ass and get your Gran's necklace back."

"Works for me." Janice mumbled a few words in Creole, and soon her hands and eyes shone with a pale, phosphorous glow. "And when we catch that *fils de pute*, I'm gonna put a gris-gris on him that's gonna make him cry for his maw-maw."

9

Despite Janice's bravado, I could tell she was nervous by the way her eyes darted around the yard. Feeling calmer than I had a right to be, I took a deep breath, exhaling slowly to further center myself as I mounted the front steps to the house. The stairs creaked in protest, and I sensed a small bit of magic being released as I mounted the porch—likely an alarm spell to let Mètminwi know he had guests.

Shit.

Knowing there was nothing for it but to forge ahead, I crossed the porch and kicked the front door down.

"Subtle much?" Janice asked as I cleared the room, sighting down the barrel of the Glock as I swept it back and forth to cover every dark corner of the foyer. The place was just what I'd expect from a haunted house, with faded and peeling wallpaper, dust-covered floors, moth-eaten Victorian-era furniture, and spiderwebs covering every sconce, chandelier, and doorway.

"He already knows we're here," I replied. "I triggered some sort of alert spell the moment my foot hit the porch steps."

"Didja' look first before you tripped the alarm?"

"Yes, but I didn't see anything. I figure this is all a construct of Mètminwi's magic, so he's going to know we're here no matter how careful we are. Best thing we can do is find the portal to his realm, get what we came for, and then beat feet before he knows what hit him."

At that exact moment, a child's laughter echoed from the second floor above us, and a door slammed somewhere nearby.

"As if," Janice muttered.

Feigning confidence I didn't feel, I shrugged. "One can hope. C'mon, I think I sense something ahead, a magical convergence of some sort. Maybe that's where we'll find Mètminwi and your necklace."

I crept forward, gun at the ready. Janice placed a hand on my shoulder, nearly causing me to jump out of my skin. She snort-chuckled and gave my neck a playful squeeze.

"Relax, tiger. Just wanted to make sure we don't lose each other in here."

"I nearly shit my pants," I whispered. "Give a guy a little warning next time, alright?"

Janice kept a hand on my shoulder as we moved through the dusty, decrepit rooms of the house. The glow from her hands gave off just enough luminescence to light the house up like day to my spell-enhanced vision. Unearthly laughter and the clinking of silverware and china echoed from somewhere deeper inside the house. I glanced back at my date, waiting until she gave me a nervous nod before continuing on.

We passed from the entry foyer into a dining room with a long, formal table that had been set with a ten-course meal. However, the food on the plates and serving ware was rotten, covered in mold and crawling with maggots. We held our breath against the smell and moved on toward a swinging door that I assumed led to the kitchen area. I heard cooking and muffled conversation on the other side of the kitchen door—loud enough to be detected, but not so that I could make out what was being said.

After counting to three on my fingers, I kicked the door open, but again we were greeted by nothing but shadows and dust. The kitchen was as empty and lifeless as the rest of the house.

"I don't know whether to be disappointed or relieved," Janice whispered.

"I'm going with relieved," I muttered over my shoulder. "This place is giving me the creeps."

"What, the mighty monster hunter has never dealt with haunts and spooks before?"

"Uh-uh, not if I could help it. Hauntings are the purview of exorcists and demonologists. I prefer my monsters to be nice and corporeal, thank you very much."

"Hmph," was Janice's only reply.

I glanced back at her. "What?"

"Oh, it's nothing."

"Janice..."

She smirked. "I just think it's cute that the great Junk-yard Druid could get riled by a haunted house."

"Ha ha, very funny." I rubbed my nose with my free hand, keeping my pistol pointed downrange. The dust was getting to me almost as much as the weird noises.

"Yeah, but you gotta admit—this date sure hasn't been boring."

"No arguments here," I whispered, creeping through the kitchen as I scanned the place using my mage-sight.

At first, I saw nothing of interest. But on my second sweep, I caught the faintest glimmer coming from a side door that was nearly hidden behind a large, old-fashioned cupboard. As I further scrutinized the doorway, lines of magic began to appear all around the door casing, the strange, curious symbols and scrollwork unique to Haitian and New Orleans voudon practice.

"I think we found our doorway," I said, pointing. "Look."

"I don't see anything," Janice said with a shake of her head. "My magic works differently than yours. Hang on a sec."

She said a few words in Creole, waving her hands around. I caught something that sounded like "reveal," and something like "keesa caché," but that was about all I could make out. Janice's hands began to glow brighter, and as they did, the faded paint began to crackle and peel from the door and frame to reveal a wrought-iron cemetery gate covered in voodoo wards and scrollwork.

The scenery beyond the gate was a surprise, although I don't know exactly what I'd expected to see. Rather than another dreary, spooky room of the house, Janice's spell had revealed a doorway to another realm, one that bore a stark resemblance to a New Orleans graveyard at night.

"When we walk through that gate, do you think we'll end up somewhere on Earth, or someplace else?" I asked with trepidation in my voice.

She shook her head. "Looks like Lafayette Cemetery, but I don't see any houses around the outskirts. I'm betting not."

"Something told me you were going to say that," I said, adjusting my baldric. Squaring my shoulders, I headed for the gate. "Alright, then. Time to make the mother-fucking beignets. Let's get this over with."

10

Any fool could see the gate was warded against entry, so I squatted in front of it, examining the spells that guarded the door to Mètminwi's realm. It didn't take me long to figure out that it was going to take some work to get the damned thing open. I was good at picking spell-locks and breaking wards, but apparently Mètminwi was even better at creating them.

"I'm going to need a minute to get this open," I said as I stood. "If you could—"

Janice pushed past me, cutting me off mid-sentence. "We don't have time for that. The doorway to Mètminwi's realm will be gone at dawn, and if we're stuck inside there when it disappears, there's no telling how long it'll be before another one opens up."

"Okay, then what are we going to do? That gate's locked up tighter than a frog's ass, and I don't have the juice to bust it down, even in my other form."

Janice looked at the gate for a moment, pursing her lips. "No need. It so happens that I have a key."

She reached into the front of her dress, pulling an old-fashioned skeleton key from her bosom.

"Okay, that's not cliché at all," I said.

"What, that I have a skeleton key, or that I pulled it out of my bra?"

"Both."

She stuck her tongue out at me. "You're just upset that you didn't get to show off by breaking through a minor god's wards."

"Yeah, well—maybe a little."

"Be glad I have the danged thing. It's how I get back and forth from Gran's house to her real digs in the under-world." She walked over to the doorway, gingerly inserting the key into a keyhole on the left side of the gate. "Let's just hope it gets us into Mètminwi's secret hideout, too."

I held my breath as she turned the key. A mechanism inside the gate clicked, and the heavy iron barrier creaked open a few inches. Janice retrieved the key and tucked it back in her bra, adjusting her cleavage absently for good measure. She frowned at the doorway, hands together as she silently tapped her fingers together in front of her chest.

In all honesty, I couldn't blame her for hesitating. We were about to tweak a minor god's nose on his own turf, after all—not exactly an advisable course of action under any circumstances. I stepped up next to her, eyes glued to the gate as I drummed up the courage to step through.

"Ahem. I suppose we'd better get a move on."

Janice gulped. "Right—adventure awaits."

"Um, do you think your Gran will come after us? I mean, once she figures out we didn't make it to the ball."

"Probably not. Nobody knows we're here but us."

I thought about all the times I'd faced down other super-baddies from The World Beneath on my own, remembering that I'd come out on top every single time. Usually by the skin of my teeth, but still.

Nobody lives forever.

"Fuck it, let's do this," I said, kicking the gate open. It swung wide, clanging against something on the other side. A cold wind blasted through the doorway, carrying the stale smell of long-decayed flesh.

"Again, subtle," Janice chided.

"Meh—he knows we're here," I said as I walked through the doorway. "May as well announce our arrival."

"Sure, now that you've told him we're coming," she groused, following me through the gate.

I ignored her, holstering my gun as I cupped my hands to my mouth. "Mètminwi! Mètminwi, show yourself, you son of a bitch. You took something that doesn't belong to you, and we're here to get it back."

Deep, rasping laughter echoed through the graveyard. "Ah, so da' druid and his little voodoo princess have arrived. Took ya' long enough."

"Yeah, well maybe if you hadn't run off like a little bitch, we wouldn't have had to chase you across town all night to get here," I said, raising my voice over the grave-yard wind that howled all around.

His laughter shook the ground. "And jes' what do you

tink yer' about to accomplish by comin' ta' ol' Mètminwi's graveyard, eh?"

"You took Gran's necklace, Mètminwi," Janice growled. "And I want it back!"

"Ah, cher," the loa boomed. "Dont'cha tink udders have tried ta' best me before? And dey failed, every last one."

Leaning over, I whispered in Janice's ear. "You see him anywhere?"

She shook her head. "Nope. It's his realm, so we won't see him unless he wants us to."

"As long as he stays hidden, we're dead in the water. If we're going to get your necklace back, I'll need you to draw him out, and then keep him busy while I shift."

She arched an eyebrow. "Does this mean I'm going to get to see your other half?"

"I'm single right now, so I'll assume you're referring to my Hyde-side."

"Oh, so that's what you call it. Sure, I'll get him to reveal himself and keep him occupied while you shift," she replied with a wicked grin. "Then you can kick his ass and get my Gran's necklace back."

"Wish me luck," I said, heading for the gate.

"Luck," she replied, then she cupped her hands to her mouth. "Stop hiding, loa, and face the music. You took what doesn't belong to you, and I intend to get it back. So, show yourself—unless you're afraid of a little ol' human *mambo* like me."

Mètminwi's face appeared out of the darkness about ten feet above where Janice stood. He smiled, pulling his taut gray skin even tighter to reveal two rows of jagged yellow teeth.

"Na' reason ta' be scared of a tiny little ting like you, priestess," he said as he leered at her. "And when I'm done wit ya', gonna drop you in my pot with da' rest of the folk I took tonight."

11

Back on the other side of the gateway in the haunted house, I'd already started my transformation. Although shifting was taking most of my attention, I managed to keep track of the interchange between Janice and the slenderman. And that conversation had now deteriorated into trading blows—metaphorically speaking, where Janice was concerned.

Mètminwi had revealed himself fully, and he'd already taken a swipe or two at my date. Janice, however, had proven to be made of sterner stuff than I might have first imagined. She deftly leapt out of the way of the loa's first strike, and managed to raise a magical barrier to block the second and subsequent blows. Her magic flashed with luminescence each time the giant slenderman's massive fists struck the dome of arcane energy she'd erected.

Yet I knew she couldn't keep it up forever, as Janice was mostly mortal and could only power a spell like that for so long. Each time the loa struck the barrier it dimmed, indicating the strain placed on my date's rapidly-depleting magical reserves. I needed to get back in the mix fast if I was going to keep her from getting squashed like a grape—and that meant focusing on finishing my transformation as quickly as possible.

Turning my full attention back to the task at hand, I monitored my transformation, observing impatiently as my bones thickened and lengthened and my muscles swelled to thrice their normal size. During this part of the change, I gained at least a few hundred pounds of mass and almost four feet in height. By the time I reached my full height, my clothes were shredded. Except my Lycra undies. They hung off me in strips as I transformed from a normal-looking human male to a nine-and-a-half-foot-tall monster.

But it wasn't just my size and mass that altered when I shifted. My right arm was now much thicker and more muscular than my left, ending in a fist that resembled a mace at the end of a tree trunk. Conversely, my left hand was shaped more like a claw, an appendage better suited to ripping and tearing flesh than it was for smashing bones.

In the final stages of the transformation, I developed a humped back, a protruding brow, and my left eye bulged out of its socket, right before my skin repaired and reformed where it had split to accommodate my increased size. And to ensure I was much more resilient and resistant to injury, my bones and flesh were much denser than in my human form. When all was said and done, I looked like Quasimodo's meaner, 'roided-out older brother—and I felt like it, as well.

Now I'm ready to rumble.

Smacking my massive right fist into my palm, I turned my attention back to what was happening on the other side of the gate.

"What happened to your friend, cher?" the giant boogeyman taunted. "He run off when ol' Mètminwi show his face, eh?"

Janice held her hands overhead, pushing with all her physical strength as well as her magical energy in an effort to maintain her shield. "Colin," she groaned, "now would be a really good time for your friend to make an appearance."

Never one to pass up the opportunity to make a timely entrance, I grabbed the edges of the door frame, forcing them wider to fit my massive shoulders. It was still a tight fit, but I somehow managed it. Once I got my upper body through, I dove into a roll—just in case Mètminwi decided to close the gate on me while I still had my legs on the other side.

As I sprang to my feet, I realized that the loa hadn't even noticed my presence, so focused was he on raining blows down on his chosen prey. Unfortunately, Janice appeared to be on her last leg. Like a comic book heroine, the magical barrier she'd cast appeared to be winking out.

With no time to spare, I yanked a tombstone from the ground, flinging it like a frisbee at Mètminwi's face. It spun through the air, striking him in the mouth where it shattered against his teeth. I couldn't be certain, but I was pretty sure the debris included at least one of his incisors.

The loa stumbled back, roaring in anger as he clasped two bony, thin-fingered hands across his mouth.

"Who dares strike Mètminwi in his own realm?" he asked. Although it came out more like, *"Who zayr strife Mah-min-me in hif oven room?"*

"I *zare*—I mean I dare!" I roared, leaping atop a rather tall mausoleum to place me as close to eye level with the thirty-foot-tall loa as possible.

"About time," Janice groused as she collapsed behind a large grave marker.

"Hey, it takes time to look this good," I stage-whispered out the side of my mouth.

By this time, Mètminwi had recovered. Although he was now missing a tooth and sporting a split lip, he appeared to be none the worse for the wear. The boogeyman pointed a long, thin finger at my chest, fixing me with eyes like two pools of darkness.

"Who ith zis, zat shallenges Mah-min-me?" he lisped, whistling his words through the gap in his front teeth.

"Say what?" I laughed, clutching my hands to my gut. "Janice, are you hearing this shit?"

"Loud and clear," she honk-snorted from her hiding place. "Sounds like someone's developed a speech impediment."

"Whaf?" Mètminwi blinked. "Do I'fe zound funny?"

"Like, crazy funny," I guffawed. "You don't hear it?"

The loa shook his head.

"Say 'espresso,'" I suggested.

"Eth-pweth-o," he replied.

Janice honk-snorted even louder while I howled like a hyena. "Hoo boy, that's a fucking riot!"

"I know, right?" Janice managed to squeal between giggle fits. "It's like, he's all scary as hell, then he opens his mouth, and..." She paused, snort-chuckling as she was overcome with another fit of laughter. Finally, she waved us off. "I can't, I just can't."

12

"Thath very cruel," the loa complained, "laughing ath thomeone's manner of speething."

"Oh, lawdy," Janice squealed, "he said 'speething'!"

"Thith ith humiliathing," the loa mumbled.

He plopped down on a mausoleum, elbows on his knees with a hangdog expression on his face. Meanwhile, Janice attempted to overcome her giggle fits, although she wisely remained hidden behind the large gravestone. I wiped my eyes and slapped my cheeks in an effort to regain some self-control and refocus on the mission.

"Okay, okay," I said, stifling a stray giggle. "I think I'm ready to fight you now. Go on, put 'em up."

"No," Mètminwi replied. "I refuth."

"Whadya mean, you 'refuth'? Need I remind you that we wouldn't be at this juncture if you hadn't sent your pet revenant to steal Janice's necklace?"

The loa gave a backhanded wave at me. "I only dith ith thoo geth Brigith's attenthun."

"Wait—what?" Janice asked, suddenly perking up. "Why'd you steal Gran's necklace again?"

"Yeah, for real—explain yourself," I said.

"Thath thing? You can haf ith," he said, reaching into his waistcoat and tossing the artifact to me. "Ith pointhleth now."

I checked the necklace in the magical spectrum. It was the genuine article. "Okay, slow down there, loverboy. You mean to tell me that you stole this necklace—and attacked my date—just so Maman Brigitte would pay attention to you?"

He nodded.

"But isn't Maman Brigitte married to Baron Samedi?" I asked, glancing at Janice for confirmation.

"True," she said, "but commitment in relationships is a bit more—fluid—among the Guédé. Gran and the Baron both have been known to take multiple lovers outside their marriage. For the most part, each looks the other way when it comes to their mutual indiscretions."

"Juth tho," Mètminwi interjected. "Ith geth lonely here, in my gwaythyard. Buth now, with thith lithp, she'll never tathe me theriothly." He began to sob, his breath whistling softly through the gap in his teeth as he did so.

Janice stood, brushing her dress off. "Aw, sug, hush now. I'm sure we can figure something out."

Janice's abrupt turnabout caused me to do a double-take. "Hang on just a minute—are you actually suggesting we help this guy?"

"Sure, why not?" she replied with a shrug.

"B-b-but—he eats children, Janice!"

Mètminwi sniffled, wiping his nose with a sheet-sized hanky he'd produced from somewhere. "Oh, you thouldn'th worry abouth thath. I thopped eathing humans ages ago. Modern dieths make them too high in cholestherol. I eath Paleo now—geth my protheen from grath-fed beeth and free-range eggth."

"See?" Janice interjected, hands on her hips. "I told you that you didn't understand the loa very well."

"Janice, you're the one who told me how evil and scary this guy was." I turned to Mètminwi, arms crossed. "Okay, so what about that revenant? Poor kid had his throat cut from ear to ear, for goodness sakes."

The loa perked up. "Huh? You mean Thylvethter? I rethcued him from an evil bokor. We've been thrying thoo find whereth the with doctor hid hith thoul, tho I can thend him on to the nexth life. Meanwhile he'th been working for me."

"Still, you attacked Janice here. I mean, you were practically trying to smash her into pulp."

He hitched a shoulder in a half-shrug. "I'th have juth spelled her to sleep and kepth her for ranthom unthil her Gran showth up. Janith wath never in any real danger."

"Ew-kaaay," I said, taking a seat on the edge of the mausoleum. "So, giant slenderman here ain't evil. Instead, he rescues murdered kids, eats only sustainably-raised meat, watches his HDL numbers—"

"LDL is the bad cholesterol," Janice said.

"Whatever. And he has a crush on your Gran."

"Thath abouth thums ith up," Mètminwi said.

"And you want to help him, after he stole your Gran's

thingamajig and attacked you?" Janice nodded, eyeing Mètminwi with a look of sympathy. "Janice, can I speak with you a moment—in private?"

I walked her to the gateway, where we huddled together as we spoke.

"You for real about this?" I asked.

"Look, Colin, I grew up around the loa. Sure, they're a little twisted, and some of them are way creepy when you compare them to gods from other pantheons. But I see them as people, just like you and me. Besides, the Baron has been more or less ignoring Gran lately. She could use a suitor to cheer her up."

I tilted my head at Mètminwi. "Him? Seriously? I mean, don't tell her I said so, but your Gran is hot. Seems like a mismatch to me."

"Meh, she has unique tastes. And she likes tall men."

I scratched my head. "Well, you got me there. Hell, now I feel bad that I knocked his tooth out."

"Don't. He took this whole thing a bit too far, so maybe it's good you brought him down a notch."

"So, how're we going to fix his lisp?"

"Well, Gran's half-brother Dian Cécht owes her a favor. Once I tell her what happened, she'll be all over getting Uncle Dian to make a new tooth for Mètminwi—on the DL, of course." She glanced over at the loa. "Poor guy's had enough blows to his ego as it is."

"Hmm... I prefer to keep my distance from the Celtic gods, so I'll let you handle all that. So long as you're sure it's safe, that is."

She looked up at me with a twinkle in her eye. "Aw, that's sweet."

"Ahem," I said, glancing around nervously. "We still have to explain to your Gran about why we missed the ball. She's gonna think I stood you up."

"Nah, don't worry about her. I'll just tell her what happened—"

"Oh, heck no—she'll kill me!"

Janice snort-laughed. "Relax, I'm kidding. But since this date got ruined, I fully expect you to follow up with another." She gave a sly wink. "And if not, well—I might just let slip how you left me to deal with Mètminwi in his own realm."

"Only for a minute!" I protested with mock indignation in my voice.

Janice shrugged, smiling.

"So, blackmail it is, eh?" I laughed. "It's a deal, then—although I can't promise how soon it'll be. My life's a little, er, crazy right now."

"Don't worry, sug," she said, resting a hand on my hairy, misshapen chest. "I know how to wait my turn."

AUTHOR'S NOTE

The next story occurs sometime during Book 8 in *The Colin McCool Paranormal Suspense Series*. There are few spoilers for the main series in this second *Blood Bound* novelette, but if you haven't yet read past Book 4, you might want to hold off on reading *Prince Mark's Price* until you do.

PRINCE MARK'S PRICE

In which the wizard Crowley does a good deed, but purely for selfish reasons...

Crowley couldn't say exactly *why* he'd taken up his comic collecting hobby, but he certainly remembered *when* it had started. A few months back, his vintage Jaguar convertible had been in the shop—it was always in the shop, but he so loved the car that he couldn't bear to part with it. Without suitable transportation, the shadow wizard had been forced to ask his annoyingly upbeat acquaintance for a ride to the grocery store so he could purchase raw meat for his familiar, the latest issue of *Martha Stewart Living*, and a sufficient volume of wine and spirits to get him through the weekend.

Of course, the mage could've sent a shadow golem to retrieve a few articles of sustenance for him, but shadow golems were stupid—and they tended to steal souls when left unattended for extended periods of time. Plus, it would have certainly brought back the wrong magazine, like *Country Home*, or *Better Homes and Gardens*, or *Magnolia*, a publication founded by that unbearably positive and kind, *nouveau riche* couple from Texas—and Crowley simply couldn't have that. So, he'd swallowed his pride then called to request that the druid pick him up at his domicile and drive him to the store.

"Can do, Crowster. But, I gotta run a few errands while we're out. Nothing major—just making a beer run, plus I have to pick up a gift for Hemi's birthday at the comic shop."

"I really don't—"

"Nonsense, it's no problem at all. Pick you up in thirty minutes."

Click.

Sigh.

Thus, Crowley had been introduced to those venerable American institutions of commerce, the convenience store and the comic book shop. Granted, he'd seen a convenience store before, but he'd never actually walked into one. The wizard preferred to pay at the pump using Speedpass, both because it was more sanitary and because it reminded him of a character from a science fiction film he'd once watched with Belladonna.

Needless to say, he was not impressed by the convenience store.

But as for the comic book shop, well—that had been another matter entirely. The place was a wreck, with no discernible rhyme or reason regarding how the various shelves and displays were laid out. It smelled like mildew, cat urine, and male teenage funk, and it was so poorly lit that the mage was forced to cast a vision-enhancing cantrip in order to read the fine print on the periodical covers.

In short, it was disgusting. But oh, the wonders that place held.

Despite the unhygienic conditions inside the shop, from the moment he cracked open an issue of *Batman: Detective Comics*, Crowley was hooked. Here was a character he could relate to—one dark, mysterious, and tragic, all at once. Yet at the same time, the detective evidenced a capacity for kindness and heroism that absolutely fascinated Crowley, as all such virtuous human motivations baffled him.

As a changeling prince, one of the few kidnapped humans fortunate enough to become a ward in servitude to a royal family in Underhill, he'd been raised as fae. Although the fae could display an intensity of emotion to match that of any human, they were altogether motivated by self-interest and nothing more. Such characteristics as empathy, compassion, and generosity were nearly unheard of, and generally were only evident in a select few of the fae's forebears, the Tuatha Dé Danann. And admittedly, even the best of the Celtic gods were mercurial and predisposed to acts of capriciousness that would make the average human sociopath gasp.

Being raised by monsters among monsters, it was no wonder that Crowley had possessed no moral compass to speak of when he'd first left Underhill. When he'd finally emerged from that harsh, cruel place, sent to Earth to do the bidding of his adoptive mother, he'd been as cold and heartless as any fae, his thoughts and motivations as alien as any other denizen of *Tír na nÓg*. It was only after several trips to Earth, necessarily rubbing elbows with humans in order to complete his assigned tasks, that he'd become fascinated by their ways.

What motivated one human to help another they barely knew? How could they sacrifice themselves in service to causes that brought them no political advancement or monetary gain? Why did they do things like feed the poor, nurse injured animals back to health, or look after their enfeebled elderly? All-in-all, humans were a mystery to him—one that occupied his thoughts both day and night.

This had ultimately led him to question his captors' infallibility, and his loyalty to them as well. Against the advice of his adoptive mother, he soon developed relationships with humans in order to learn more about them. Finally, he fell in love with a human woman, discovering emotions within that he never realized he possessed.

Then the druid had bested him—through sheer luck, no less—and his adoptive father had refused him succor as punishment for his failure. That was the last straw, and when Crowley finally turned his back on the fae, he'd done so for good. Although his decision meant he'd be looking over his shoulder for the rest of his life, at least he was finally free.

But that decision had led to even greater and more perplexing challenges. Now, he had to learn how to live among his own people—a race so foreign to him he may as well have been visiting Earth from a distant galaxy. And he craved human contact, no matter how he tried to deny it.

These were urges he did not fully understand, and they most certainly explained why comic book stories of anti-heroes and villains, tragedy and saviors, moral dilemmas and clear-cut choices appealed to him so.

Although he'd be hard-pressed to put it into words, Crowley was learning to be human by reading comics. That was why he was currently browsing the aisles of a disgustingly unsanitary comic book store, looking for original copies of *Detective Comics* #575–578. Sure, he could read them online, but the digital versions simply didn't appeal to Crowley. They denied him of the sensory experience that made printed comics so uniquely enjoyable.

No, he preferred to purchase them here, at his chosen comic book store. Distasteful and banal as it was, nobody bothered him in this place, because the owner could care less about such trivial human concerns as being helpful and providing a positive customer experience. Crowley had visited other, tidier shops, but unfortunately they had employees who spoke to him—and that was something he simply could not abide. For that reason alone, Prince Mark's had become his favorite place to find new comics to read.

Thus, this was now *his* comic book store. And if the owner had something dark, evil, and magical hidden in the basement, it was none of Crowley's concern. All he cared about was finding his damned comic books.

14

If there was one thing Theo loved, it was going to Prince Mark's. Prince Mark's, also known as Prince Mark's Comic & Game Emporium, was the one place where he could escape from his life. Escape from being bullied at school, from being ignored by his shitty stepmother (who only paid attention to him when his dad was in town), and from living in a new town where he had very few friends and virtually no social skills that would allow him to change that situation.

It was no wonder that Theo wasn't very popular. Being the new kid was hard enough, but what made it even harder was that he really didn't stand out for being exceptional at anything at all. He wasn't very good at sports—although he had taken up karate recently—but he could barely catch a ball, never mind dribble, throw a spiral, or run a lay-up. As for schoolwork, he was bright but uninterested, and thus made mediocre grades. And where girls were concerned? Well, Theo was even more awkward around them than he was around everyone else.

But at Prince Mark's, Theo could be somebody else. There, no one cared about whether you could dunk, or if you got to second base with Molly Steward (everyone said she was a slut, but Theo had always thought she was very nice), or if you were in the National Honor Society. Those things mattered little to the denizens of Pflugerville's one and only comic book store. No, the only thing the kids at Prince Mark's cared about was, did you know comics?

If you did, you were in. Knowing your shit when it came to comic books was a ticket to the cool kid's group for sure. And Theo wanted in that group more than he wanted anything else in life, or perhaps ever. Even more than he wanted his parents to get back together, although he would be ashamed to admit it. Because really, he just wanted to fit in somewhere for once in his life.

There was a group of older kids at Prince Mark's that got to hang out in the basement, where the owner, Richard, supposedly had all this cool stuff stashed. The basement entrance was hidden by a purple curtain, directly behind the front counter where Richard was almost permanently ensconced. Theo couldn't remember a time when he'd entered the comic shop when the owner wasn't sitting like a hawk behind the cash register, reading some obscure graphic novel like *SCUD* or *Technopriests*.

If the rumors were true, it was no wonder that Richard guarded the basement door like a sphinx. Beyond that velvet drape were said to be treasures beyond imagining: ultra-rare comic books, medieval weapons, and a gaming table full of set props and painted miniatures that was said to be as big as Jimmy Seacamp's bedroom. But Theo hadn't been invited to hang out in the basement yet. In fact, he feared he'd never be invited behind the purple curtain, ever.

A month back, he'd been well on his way to earning admittance to the august company of cool kids who hung out at Prince Mark's. Richard was known to ignore kids who shopped there, but it was said that if you came around often enough, and long enough, eventually he'd test you. He'd start by asking you questions about the comics you liked, why you liked them, and so on; and if he liked what he heard, he'd start asking you about obscure comic book trivia. Pass Richard's tests, and like that, you'd be in like Flynn.

Weeks ago, Richard started asking Theo questions when he'd come in to pick up the latest issues of his favorite series. When Richard noticed an issue of *Moon Knight* in the stack, he asked Theo who he thought would win in a fight between Batman and Moon Knight. The young man replied a bit too quickly, saying that obviously they could never fight, since one character was from the DC universe and the other from the Marvel universe.

This had earned him a deep frown from his inquisitor.

But when Theo followed up by saying it would depend on Marc Spector's psychological stability at the time, and whether the moon was full or not, he received a grunt and a nod of grudging respect. The next time Theo came into the store, the boy felt Richard watching him as he perused the stacks. As he was leaving, the store owner stopped him on his way out.

"Some of the older kids have a D&D campaign going on Thursday nights, in the room in back. You should come."

Theo gave a nod and said he'd consider it, barely keeping his cool as he walked out the door. But as soon as he was down the block, he screamed his lungs out, laughing and jumping up and down like a madman. People stared, but he didn't care. He was on his way into the cool kid's group.

That was, until the fateful night when he showed up to the game. Rhone, the de facto leader of the group, had at first tried to turn him away. But when he heard that Richard had invited Theo, he quickly relented.

"Alright, you can stay and play. The group needs a cleric anyway, since Rob is out with the flu. But you'll have to roll a character from scratch—no re-rolls, either. Sheets are over there. Write it up so we can get started."

Theo pulled his dice from his bag, along with some Xeroxed sheets of paper and a pencil. "I have my own."

"Fine." Rhone turned back to the table to resume scheming with the rest of the party on how they were going to take out an ogre that was guarding the entrance to the dungeon. As an afterthought, he called to Theo over his shoulder. "No cheating, kid—trust us, we'll know."

Theo didn't cheat when he rolled his character, and that was a fact. But when he rolled three natural eighteens, a seventeen, a fourteen, and a ten, well—it was pretty much a given that the cool kids wouldn't believe him. He didn't realize it at the time, and simply figured they'd think it was boss that he'd rolled such good stats.

Instead, they'd branded him a cheater and banned him from the gaming room for life. Now he was a pariah, an outcast at Prince Mark's. But Theo had a plan, one that would almost guarantee that the cool kids would have to accept him back into their clique.

All he had to do was sneak past the purple curtain to do it.

15

Crowley noticed the child lurking just out of sight because he was clearly trying *not* to be noticed, and that immediately drew the wizard's attention. It was habit for him to perceive anything that didn't want to be seen, because so many hidden things in Underhill could kill you.

His mother's assassins were also known to disguise themselves as innocuous-looking humans, especially since the direct approach to capturing him had proven to be lethal to the first few retrieval teams she'd sent. Lugh knew how many little old ladies, blind beggars, and Boy Scouts the mage had incinerated, eviscerated, dismembered, and otherwise disposed of in gruesome and ruthless ways lately. Of course, they hid in order to take the wizard unawares, and also because the sight of a tall, dark, brooding man with facial scars attacking an elderly woman tended to draw a crowd. And as far as his adoptive mother was concerned, the more trouble she could cause for her former ward, the better.

In fact, it had cost the shadow mage a small fortune in gold to pay off Maeve's fixers, since Fuamnach's killers had become more and more brazen with every attempt. When they'd first come after him they'd done it in secret, waiting until he was alone before they attacked. But now they were past that, and the kid gloves were off.

Generally speaking, Crowley could neutralize the odd witness without injuring them too badly, but mind magic wasn't his strong suit. And after he'd flubbed a mind-wipe, Maeve had insisted that he call professional help to clean up after each clash with Fuamnach's people. Personally, he couldn't see why Maeve had been upset. So he'd accidentally caused a fifty-two-year-old stockbroker to mentally revert back to age ten—it wasn't like he'd killed the man, after all.

Or, worse, allowed a witness to blab on social media about magic and elves and the like. That was the cardinal sin, and it could easily result in Crowley falling from the good graces of Queen Maeve. If that ever happened, he'd have to move away from Belladonna—and that simply wouldn't do. No, he'd gladly pay well for help in cleaning up his messes because he liked this city, and he had very good reason to stay.

Still, he'd prefer to avoid making a scene here if he could manage it. The child looked harmless enough—a chubby, blank-faced boy with thick glasses, a huge afro, and too-large feet that likely made him clumsier than that oaf of a druid apprentice who called himself Crowley's "frenemy." But looks could be deceiving, so the mage kept an eye on him, ready to pull the child into a lonely alcove or restroom and terminate with prejudice, should he reveal himself to be an actual threat.

Surprisingly, the more the wizard watched the boy, the more it became clear that he wasn't interested in Crowley at all. He was instead monitoring the fat slob of a man who owned the store. Why he was so fascinated by the slovenly cretin was not quite clear, as the fellow was a boor with the personal hygiene habits of an alcoholic hagfish. He smelled of beer and sausage and unwashed skin, he almost always had the remnants of his last meal in his beard and mustache, and he sometimes broke wind while customers were in the store.

On top of all that, he leered at the teenage girls who occasionally visited the shop. Crowley was exceptionally prejudiced against adults who were attracted to children, for reasons that were, shall we say, *personal* to him. More than once the mage had considered disintegrating the man on principle. The comic shop would close if he did, and that had stayed his hand—but he revisited the decision from time to time, especially when the man engaged in public eructation.

As for the boy, the mage became convinced he was no threat at all and decided to pay him no mind. He was just a child, after all, and children constantly did things that made absolutely no sense to Crowley. So, he went back to flipping through back issues of Batman and Moon Knight, dismissing the matter entirely.

That was, until the ruckus started.

At first Crowley thought it was gunfire, but then he recognized the sound. Someone had fired off a package of fireworks directly in front of the store, close enough to rattle the door and shake the front glass. A childish prank, no more, and nothing that concerned the wizard. However, it attracted the attention of the store owner, who jumped off his stool and hobbled around the counter to see what had caused the racket.

No sooner had the store owner exited the door than the boy darted out of his hiding place, heading for the front of the store. Initially, the wizard thought he was headed for the cash register—a petty thief in the making, for sure. Or perhaps he meant to steal one of the rare collectibles that the owner kept on display behind the counter. Either way, it was none of Crowley's business, and he only noted the child's actions out of habit.

But when the boy took a sharp left turn to duck behind that garish curtain, bypassing the register and merchandise both, Crowley's curiosity was piqued. To his eyes, the draped doorway stood out as plain as day, but to the other people who entered the store it may as well have been invisible. That's because someone had cast a strong look-away, forget-me spell on that section of wall, presumably because the owner kept something hidden in the basement that was not meant for public consumption.

So how did the child know the doorway was there? And, how did he know the store owner would be distracted at that moment, providing the boy with the opportunity to sneak past the curtain? Could it be that the child had caused the disturbance outside as an intentional diversion, so that he might see whatever lay beyond the doorway?

If so, the child was much more than he appeared. Perhaps he was in league with someone who wanted the foul, mysterious thing hidden below—a mage, witch, or necromancer. Was the child being forced to steal it? Certainly it wasn't just childish curiosity, because then how would he have seen past the glamour cast on the door?

If he was a mundane child and not someone clued in on The World Beneath, that boy was in serious danger. Should he disturb whatever the store owner kept locked away beneath his shop, he'd likely not survive the encounter. Missing children tended to bring police, who would in turn suspect the owner, who might possibly be jailed...

... and then, no more comic books for Crowley.

"Drat," he cursed under his breath. Without another word, he cast a concealment spell on himself and slipped behind the curtain.

16

Theo's heart beat in his chest as he made his descent, pounding out a steady "whoomp-whoomp-whoomp," a testament to the fact that the boy needed to get more exercise. Yet it wasn't just the short sprint through the store that had his heart aflutter; he was excited about the prospects of what he might find below, and more than a little scared that he might be caught. Outside of being reprimanded for reading comics during Mrs. Wamble's class, and that time he knocked his stepmom's ceramic owl collection over while playing Star Wars in the house, Theo had never been in trouble in his life.

The stairs creaked with his every step, loudly enough that anyone in the store upstairs would hear him trespassing. Thankfully, there'd only been one other person in the store, and that dude had his head so deep in the stacks Theo doubted he even paid him any mind. And he hadn't yet heard the front door chime, so he knew that Richard was likely still investigating the source of the noise.

It was a simple trick, really, one Theo had designed so it removed all evidence of wrongdoing once sprung. He'd taken one of his stepmom's cigarettes, torn the filter off, and poked a wick-sized hole through one end, as close to the tip as possible. Then, he'd unwrapped a package of firecrackers, stuck the fuse through the hole, and lit the cigarette, hiding the makeshift time bomb carefully beneath the old-school mailbox that sat in front of Prince Mark's. After a short jaunt down the street and back, he'd entered the store as invisibly as he always did these days, in plain sight but ignored by Richard and everyone else of consequence.

Amazingly, it had worked. Theo had finally pierced the veil and was about to see if the rumors were true. And if they were, he'd put his plan into effect. Like the time bomb distraction device, his scheme was simple yet ingenious. He would steal Richard's most valuable comics, such as the *Amazing Fantasy* #15 and *Tales of Suspense* #39 he was rumored to have locked away in the basement. There were also supposed to be three copies of *Avengers* #1 down here, but that was no big deal. Still, he'd snag those too, just because he wanted to flip through one of them—only if it was GD quality or below, mind you.

And then he'd wait a few weeks, biding his time until things cooled down and Richard lost hope of ever getting his prized collectible editions back. At that point, Theo would show up saying he'd found the comics in a dumpster. Then, the cool kids would know he wasn't a cheat and Richard would insist they accept the younger boy into their peer group. He'd be a hero.

It was the perfect plan, and Theo was already halfway there. Now, he just had to follow through and snag those rare comics. That is, if the rumors were true.

As he reached the bottom of the stairs he paused, hiking his backpack higher on his shoulders. Then he closed his eyes and took a deep breath before rounding the corner into the room beyond.

"Holy shit," he whispered when he first saw the place. "Those assholes were telling the truth."

The room ahead was rather large, perhaps twenty by twenty feet. The walls were cinder block, painted in murals that depicted fantasy scenes and famous comic book cells. The artwork had been expertly done in crisp lines and vibrant colors, so the characters and creatures portrayed seemingly jumped off the wall in 3D.

In addition to the artwork, the place was a geeky kid's paradise. Old-school arcade games and pinball machines lined one wall and beanbag chairs were scattered here and there, as well as a huge, comfy-looking leather couch. In the corner sat a soda machine that had "FREE" written on a piece of white tape that covered the price sign. Even better, if the button labels were for real, the machine was filled with Jolt cola.

But that wasn't the most amazing thing about the room.

No, the feature that jumped out at Theo was the huge gaming table that served as the centerpiece. Jaw-droppingly large, it was probably bigger than his bedroom, and a heck of a lot cooler. Easily fifteen feet long and almost as wide, the surface was chalkboard green with pale gray grid lines marking it from one end to the other.

Currently, it looked to be set up for a dungeon module. Much of it had been overlaid with map layouts that depicted an underground complex of caves, tunnels, and sewers, all as artfully depicted as the wall murals. Painted miniatures were set up all over the board, as if someone had been planning out a campaign and deciding where to hide all the monsters and villains. And, to top it all off, a set of chrome-plated metal dice sat atop a black crush velvet bag at one end, next to a leather dungeon master's screen that had been folded flat.

Theo slowly walked around the table, taking it all in and committing the sight to memory. He might not be back this way, as his plan required him to leave the shop without being seen. So, he wanted to make sure he remembered this perfectly; that way, he could play it cool when Richard invited him down here.

But this wasn't what he'd come to find. With a reluctant sigh, Theo tightened his backpack straps and headed into the next room.

17

"Honestly, who lives like this?" Crowley muttered as he carefully picked his way down the stairs. Every step was strewn with garbage and debris, the detritus of a modern underachiever's depraved lifestyle. Beer cans, soda bottles, cellophane wrappers, empty potato chip bags, pornographic magazines—it was enough to make the wizard vomit.

And spider webs—ugh, how he hated spider webs. It wasn't that he was afraid of them; it was just that their silk tended to cling to one's clothing, and the wizard hated to present an unkempt appearance. Crowley torched the thin gray strands with a snap of his fingers as he picked his way down the stairs, careful to avoid puddles and stains that were potentially suspect.

"Oh, for the sake of all that's dark and unholy," he hissed as he stepped in something soft and squishy that clung to his shoe.

They were Berluti's, and possibly ruined now. Thankfully, he had two more pairs just like them, but it still irked him that he'd have to get in his car and drive home wearing soiled shoes. Unfortunately, the unique nature of Crowley's magic meant that it was great for destroying things, but not so useful for fixing them. The last time he'd tried to clean a pair of shoes with magic, his tower had smelled of burnt leather for days. Cleaning a pair of shoes by hand was simply out of the question, so into the trash they would go.

"That child had best not trigger a deadly curse or release a denizen of the lower realms of hell before I find him. Because if he does, I'm going to raise him from the dead and then kill the little guttersnipe all over again for making me follow him down here."

Before he'd headed down, Crowley had paused just inside the doorway to examine the look-away, forget-me spell that had been placed on it. Interestingly, the wards and runes had been crafted in such a way that the spell was attuned specifically to adults. Which, of course, explained how the child was able to see the basement entrance—but not why the store owner would want to keep such a secret from his adult patrons only.

Unless...

That would make sense, since the shopkeep did seem to have deviant tendencies. It was something Crowley would have to look into, once he prevented the boy from dying a horrible death and getting his favorite comic book shop shut down. Perhaps the wizard could hire a doppel-gänger to replace the man, and then purchase the shop through one of the many shell corporations he owned. It wasn't as if he hadn't done such things before. Doppel-gängers were difficult to find, however, so the wizard would prefer to keep it in the hands of the current owner.

Once he'd shaken as much offal from his shoe as possible, the shadow wizard proceeded to the bottom of the stairs only to find that the basement was flooded, inches deep. Cursing the boy, his parents, and seven generations of his offspring, the mage stepped into the fetid, stagnant water and forged ahead. A dark cinder-block doorway to his left was the only way forward, and he was about to step through when he noticed something *off* about the entrance.

"Well, well—someone has been very, very naughty," he said, crossing his arms and tapping a finger on his chin as he considered the trap wards that had been laid on the threshold.

Again, these wards were specifically attuned to trigger only if they were crossed by someone of the adult persuasion. The casting itself was nothing to note—a simple spell-trap that any second-year magic student could disarm. However, the sheer power that had been woven into it and the nefariousness of the effects were something to behold.

If Crowley had passed into the next room, he'd have been instantly frozen to negative 100 degrees Celsius, then hit with an impact spell that was roughly equivalent to being struck by a fast-moving semi-truck. Once he lay shattered in pieces on the floor, he'd have been sprayed with an ultra-caustic acid, which in turn would have turned his remains into sludge.

Knowing this, the wizard reassessed his decision to tromp through the rank expanse of water that covered the floor. Upon closer inspection, there were things floating in the murk that might've been human bones. He'd have been impressed, if he weren't so revolted by the untidiness of it all.

Still, he had to give the caster a grudging amount of respect. As he disarmed the trap and neutralized the spell, Crowley resolved to proceed more carefully thereafter. Such caution would require that he moved at a much more leisurely pace as well, because one never hurried when entering another mage's sanctuary—no matter how meager the presiding magic-user's skills.

It was a tough break for the child, however. He'd likely run afoul of the evil presence that lurked ahead long before Crowley caught up to him. There was nothing to be done for it, but the upside was that the wizard wouldn't have to converse with the child upon rescuing him.

He was happily counting his lucky stars when he remembered that was precisely the outcome he wished to prevent. With a sigh, the wizard cast an illumination spell, then trudged off into the darkness while cursing the druid for introducing him to such a plebeian, philistine hobby in the first place.

18

The next room after the gaming room was a sight to behold, causing Theo to pause and take his time to explore it thoroughly. The walls were stone—whether fake or real, the boy could only guess—and the ceiling arched, like the inside of an old church he'd once visited with his grandma. Electric chandeliers hung from thick iron chains overhead, lighting the place from corner to corner so each and every feature could be fully appreciated.

And oh, what wondrous sights this room held. It was set up like a museum, with glass cases spaced apart in a grid pattern so that the room was laid out in aisles and rows. The displays were roped off, and each aisle was marked by its own red carpet that led to the next exhibit.

Inside those cases were an array of period weaponry, armor, and clothing, the likes of which young Theo had never before seen. Clearly labeled by tent cards and brass placards, each explained what the items were as well as where and when they were from. There were suits of armor from the Middle Ages, swords from every period and nation, shields, maces, morningstars, crossbows, lances, spears, and even a trident or two, which the signs indicated to be Roman in origin.

"How in the heck did Richard get all this stuff?" Theo wondered aloud as he strolled the aisles, open-mouthed.

For a moment, he considered that the comic book shop owner might be a Bruce Wayne type—or a Connor MacLeod, at least. However, he quickly dismissed that idea on the grounds that he rarely saw Richard move from his stool behind the counter. Still, there had to be a reason he kept all that weaponry and armor down here. Maybe he sold antique weapons and stuff on the side, to support his comic book habit?

Speaking of which, Theo had a job to do, and now he wanted to complete that task more than ever. The wonders of the basement rooms beneath Prince Mark's had proven to be far beyond even his wildest imaginings, and he couldn't wait to be able to enjoy them at his leisure. With a heavy sigh, Theo bade farewell to the displays, then he hurried on to see what the next chamber might hold in store.

To enter that room, the boy had to open one-half of a pair of massive steel and wood doors. They were the type you might expect to see inside a castle or dungeon, made from dark wood clad in hammered iron, with studded rivets and handles that clanged when you released them. When he finally managed to yank the door open—which took considerable effort and not a small amount of inadvertent farting—he had to admit that the resulting view was a bit disappointing.

"What the hell, man—a book? Seriously?"

The room ahead was dark, lit only in the center by a single light that shone down upon a pedestaled display case, not unlike the ones Theo had seen in the previous room. Shadows played at the corners of his vision as he entered, as if things were moving in the dark that did not want to be seen. He almost turned back, but there was something about the book inside the case that made him take another step... and one after that... and the next until he stood in front of the case.

"Whoa."

The book had been left laid open, revealing thick, yellowed parchment pages that had been written in a harsh, angular script unlike anything Theo had ever seen. Except perhaps in a Dungeons & Dragons manual, or on a high fantasy novel cover. As he stared at them, the letters began to swim and blur, causing him to avert his eyes.

Wait—was it his imagination, or had he begun to understand what it said?

The boy looked at the pages again, steeling himself to keep his eyes focused on those weird symbols even after they'd begun to shift and change shape. He soon grew nauseous and broke out in a cold sweat, and the hair stood up on his arms. But then, the words reformed before his eyes. Their meaning became somewhat readable, if still gibberish:

SORCERIE AND CONJURESON FOR ENPRISONMENT OF DEOFLES

"Cool."

It was beyond a doubt the absolute best D&D prop Theo had ever seen. Obviously there was some sort of hidden camera, projecting words and images onto the pages from above, perhaps in the light overhead? He wished he had time to figure out how it worked, but he had to get a move on if he was to find those comics and get out of here in time for supper.

Theo trudged toward the door ahead. This entrance was much more mundane than the last, simply a plain wooden door with a glass handle and nothing more. The boy swung it open wide and out flooded warm, soft light that blinded him with its glow. But as his eyes adjusted to the glare within, he could soon make out the details of the room beyond.

"Jackpot," he whispered.

His eyes slowly swept across the space in front of him, taking in every detail so he could remember this moment forever. It was a sitting room, one meant for reading and nothing more, filled with soft, comfortable chairs, plush carpets, side tables, reading lamps, and shelf after shelf of comics in clear cellophane slipcovers. There were books as well, fantasy novels and grimdark, steampunk and contemporary, modern and classics—but it was the comics that caught Theo's eye.

Specifically the shelf with a half-dozen or so older, slightly yellowed copies encased in Lexan display boxes, standing face out for all to see. This was the holy grail—Theo had found his prize. He was just about to start stuffing cases in his bag when a low groan came from a chair to his left.

He spun quickly, landing in an awkward crouch, only to find that the source of that noise appeared to be dozing —with a comic in his lap, no less. It was, of all people, his nemesis Rhone. The teen had drool running down his chin, and he was dirty and disheveled in a manner that Theo had never before seen. There was also something on his shirt.

"Is that... blood?"

19

"Oh, now that is foully done," the wizard observed as he turned the corner from the stairwell into the room ahead.

The glamour had been subtly cast—obviously not the work of the amateur who'd trapped the stairs, mind—and artfully attuned so it would only appear in the presence of someone who had not yet reached adulthood. It was quite the illusion, and he applauded the deviousness of whoever had woven that spell.

Essentially, the caster had created the perfect honey trap—a paradisiacal wonderland specifically designed to ensorcell unsuspecting youths. The nature of the illusion, as well as the unique signature of the magic itself, told the mage much about what he might be up against. The danger was worth noting, and he'd be ready should he run afoul of the author.

Crowley was unconcerned, as he'd dealt with this kind before. However, he paused to make a few preparations for propriety's sake, shifting his magical energies and shoring up his defenses as well. Even the lowest imp could be dangerous when cornered in its lair, just as it was wise to respect even a simple hedge witch in her sanctuary.

The wizard proceeded with caution as he moved through the room, watching out for other traps and keeping a careful eye for stacked illusions. Eldritch entities who were skilled at casting glamours would often layer them, one atop the other, in an attempt to deceive those who might pierce the most obvious façade. Inexperienced mages often fell prey to such simple tricks, their pride swollen at having spotted one illusion while another they hadn't noticed would conceal their doom.

It was fortunate that Crowley knew that trick, because several such inveiglements were scattered throughout the rooms, each designed to trigger only in the presence of an adult, and every one more deadly than the last. He found and deactivated no less than three decapitation spells, two disintegration rays, one conjuration that would summon three demons from the third level of hell, and a pair of combination fireball and lightning spells with enough energy to easily fry an ogre down to ash and bone fragments.

Obviously, Richard the shopkeep had a vested interest in keeping nosy adults out of his business. Crowley considered this, and hoped that he wouldn't have to create a dimensional vortex to banish the symbiote that had given the slob his powers. Dimensional vortices were quite difficult to cast, and when the wizard taxed the limits of his magical reserves, there were consequences.

If that were to happen, the boy wouldn't survive regardless of his intentions. Then, the whole sordid affair would be for naught and he'd have to find another place to purchase his comics. Or—foulness forbid—he'd have to resort to that soulless practice of shopping online. No, that simply wouldn't do. It was best to avoid resorting to the magical equivalent of the nuclear option, if he could help it.

It wasn't long before Crowley came to the only room in the basement that wasn't flooded. The floor had been raised in that area, because it was where the magician performed dark magic. Rudimentary magic, but evil and forbidden nonetheless. Of course, that room contained the shopkeep's grimoire, a surprisingly powerful artifact that the shadow wizard was certain had not been written by that fat slob of a man.

For one, the tome was too old. It had been originally written in ancient Sumerian, but the spellbook was ensorcelled so it could be read by anyone with a smidgen of magical affinity in the reader's own language. The ensorcellment hadn't been updated in a few centuries, however, and when Crowley looked at the grimoire it was written in Middle English.

Upon reading the page to which the book had been left open, the wizard began to chuckle. It seemed that Richard had been attempting to summon and capture another entity, most likely to enslave it and increase his power. It was the classic beginner's mistake, one many a fledgling magician had succumbed to over the millennia. When you made a deal with the devil, the devil didn't share. And once an enchantress or sorcerer made one too many deals with the wrong entities, their life became forfeit.

"Imbecile," the wizard muttered.

Despite the lack of wit on the part of the grimoire's current owner, the tome still had great worth for someone of Crowley's talents. He was tempted to take it then and there, but the shopkeep had set safeguards and alarms on the book that would take the mage hours to defuse. If things went the way he expected they might, there would be ample time later to retrieve the spell tome.

For now, he'd focus on the boy, and then come back for the book once his task was done. That way, at least, the trip wouldn't be a complete waste of his time. This place could also easily function as a perfectly serviceable hideaway should his mother's henchmen discover where he'd been hiding. All the more reason to find the boy and deal with the entity and its master.

Of course, he'd be forced to find a doppelgänger or fetch to supplant the shopkeep, as that simply could not be helped at this juncture. But on the plus side, Crowley could easily assign Borovitz and Feldstein to acquire the property for him on the sly, saving him the trouble of doing it personally. Then he'd have gained another hide-out, and kept his favorite comic shop in business to boot.

Best rescue that boy, then.

With one last longing look at the grimoire, the shadow mage strode off to find the child.

20

Theo tiptoed over to the teen so as not to wake him. Using the lightest touch possible, he gently pulled the collar of the youth's shirt down to expose the wound on his chest. What the boy saw gave him chills.

Teeth marks. Just what in the actual pluckity-pluck is going on here?

Things were starting to smell very rotten in Denmark to Theo, and as his suspicions grew, he began to realize that this was all very, very wrong. Nobody had rooms and treasures and valuable collectibles like this except billionaires, and they certainly didn't keep their stuff in basements under rundown comic book shops. The whole experience had an almost dreamlike quality to it, making him wonder if both he and Rhone hadn't been drugged somehow.

That's when he got scared.

"Rhone, wake up," he said as he jostled the teen. "C'mon, man, open your eyes."

After a few unsuccessful attempts at gently waking his nemesis, Theo grabbed the older boy by the shoulders and shook him with force. But no matter how hard he tried, the teenager would simply not wake up.

"Leave him be, child. The young man merely sleeps."

Theo spun around, his eyes darting back and forth as they swept across the room. The voice was silky smooth and strangely accented—Russian maybe, but different. It had spoken in a calm, unhurried manner, but Theo detected an oily, sinister undercurrent beneath the mild words that made his spine tingle.

"Sh-show yourself," the boy demanded, feeling a lot less sure of himself than even his shaky voice might indicate.

"Why, I'm right behind you," the voice said.

The boy turned, and sure enough, there was a strange little man standing behind him. He was shorter than Theo and barrel-chested, with thin stumpy legs, too-long arms, and a round, bald skull that had just a few wisps of gray hair at the top. His face was short and wide, with high cheekbones, very little chin to speak of, and a broad mouth with thin frog lips stretched wide in a predator's smile that showed just enough teeth to threaten.

"Who are you?" Theo asked.

"Gazsi, but you can call me Gaz. And you are?"

"I wouldn't give him your name," another voice said, this one soft, confident, and dangerous.

Gaz and Theo both turned to see who'd spoken, and there in the doorway stood a tall, thin, athletically-built man with dark, wavy hair, a scarred face, and a brooding expression. He wore expensive clothes, like a model on the cover of a men's style magazine, and he leaned against the doorframe with his arms crossed, exuding cocky arrogance. Theo didn't know if he liked this guy any more than he did Gaz, because frankly they both looked dangerous and evil in their own ways.

"I don't have to listen to you," the boy said for lack of a better response.

"That's true," the tall man said, "but if you lose your soul, don't say I didn't warn you."

"Pfah, he lies," Gaz said. "I work for Richard, caring for his collection and artifacts, and ensuring that these rooms are kept in good repair."

"You talk funny," Theo remarked. "Like someone who isn't used to talking to normal people."

"That's because he isn't a normal person," the tall man replied. "Or a person at all."

"Silence, trespasser!" Gaz screamed. "Leave the child to make his own decision, or I'll be forced to deal with you directly."

The man's eyebrow twitched upward, ever so slightly. "Yawn."

"What decision?" Theo asked.

"Why, the most important decision of all, child. To have your greatest wishes granted, your grandest desires fulfilled. To be liked and respected by your peers, to be loved by your paramour, to have the world at your fingertips," Gaz said. "Or, to remain what you are—a loser, a nobody, a has-been."

"Oh, to be washed up at age eleven," the tall man interjected as he examined his fingernails. "How will the child ever recover from the raw deal he's been dealt, I wonder?"

Theo's face scrunched up as he frowned in consternation. "What's a paramour?"

"No need to worry about that, young one. Suffice it to say that, if you wanted one, you'd have it." A long, thin tongue darted out to wet the corner of Gaz's mouth, making him appear even more frog-like. "All you have to do is ask."

"There ain't no free lunch—at least, that's what my dad always says." Theo scratched the base of his neck, which always itched when he was nervous. "So, what do you get in return?"

"A small thing, only. Nothing you'd miss," Gaz replied.

"Surely you're not this stupid," the man said. "If you are, I'll gladly allow you to suffer the consequences of your idiocy. One less imbecile to dilute the human gene pool."

"Begone, magician!" Gaz screeched. "I'll not warn you again."

The man pushed off the doorframe and stood to his full height. "Silence, imp. You're not speaking to some mortal peasant, but a prince of Underhill."

"A changeling prince from the looks of it," Gaz responded, "and not one born of royal blood."

"But a prince nonetheless—trained by the Black Sorceress herself," the tall man replied, causing Gaz to shrink into himself a bit. "You'd be wise to desist, before I lose my patience and show you what her royal highness revealed to me in the many years I spent under her most thorough tutelage."

The small, strange man considered his options for a moment, then made a weird little bowing motion. "As you wish, master prince."

"As I thought. The boy is coming with me."

"What about Rhone?" Theo asked, figuring he was better off leaving with the man, since he could always ditch him later.

"Never mind him. He made his choice, and we can't take him with us." The tall man pointed a finger at Gaz, fixing him with a stern look. "Warn your master of our passing, and I will kill you. Come, boy, it's time to leave."

The man turned and left the room without even glancing back to see if Theo followed. The boy took one last look at Rhone, then shrugged and scurried to follow as quickly as his legs would carry him.

21

C rowley looked down at the boy walking next to him. "You were smart to come with me."

"What would have happened if I'd stayed? Would I have ended up like Rhone?"

"Perhaps you're not as dense as you first appeared." The wizard glanced around before fixing his gaze on his companion. "Stick close, and you might live to see tomorrow."

"That's a joke, right?"

"No, I rarely jest." Crowley headed for the pedestal that held the grimoire, and the boy scurried along beside him.

"My name's Theo," the boy said.

"I don't need to know your name," Crowley replied. "And you don't need to know mine. You won't remember anything after this is all done, anyway."

"Why not?"

Crowley stopped in front of the book, arms crossed. "Quiet. I need to think."

"You gonna steal that book? Why not just smash the glass and go?"

Crowley kept his eyes on the book and stand, busy finding the various alarm spells and traps that protected it. He set his mouth in a grim line as his eyes followed the various weaves. It would take some time to determine what they did and how he might defuse them.

"First off, there is no glass. What you're seeing is an illusion."

Theo rolled his eyes. "Whatever. I can see it right there. Look, if I rap on the glass—"

"Don't!" Crowley reached out to stop him, but it was too late. The boy's hand touched the grimoire, triggering a silent alarm spell. "Well, now you've done it."

"Whoa, that's weird. I swear there was a glass case around that thing just a second ago. Then I touched it and it disappeared."

The wizard grabbed him by the shirtsleeve, slowly pulling him away from the book. "Don't touch anything else, not unless I tell you to do so. It's fortunate that he's been feeding children to that *lidérc*, because most of the grimoire's protection spells are attuned to adults and not children. That being said, if you had tried to abscond with the book, you'd have been fried on the spot. Regardless, he's now been alerted to our presence. No doubt he'll arrive shortly to investigate."

"What do you mean, fried? And who's been feeding kids to—what did you say again?"

"A lidérc. It's an imp that feeds on a person, slowly stealing their soul in exchange for temporary magical power. It normally kills its master over time, but apparently Richard found a way to make a deal with it. He's likely been feeding it children to keep it from killing him. Rather ingenious, actually. Why no one ever thought of doing such a thing before is a mystery."

"You're saying that Gaz dude is a la dork."

"Lidérc. It's Hungarian for incubus."

"Now there's a word I know," Theo said. "Medium fiend. Neutral evil, shapechanger, AC 15, 12d8+12 hit points, and resistant to just about everything but magical weapons. Draining Kiss is their deadliest spell. Not to be messed with, unless you have a lot of protection from evil scrolls."

Crowley's brow furrowed. "I only understood about half of what you said, but yes, they are dangerous if you have no knowledge of defensive magic."

"Oh, is that why you want the spellbook? I mean, if it's real and stuff."

"It's real, whether you choose to believe or not. How did you know what it is?"

The boy shrugged. "I read it. Wasn't that hard—I just had to stare at it for a while without puking."

The wizard pursed his lips. "Interesting. But no, I have my own magic. Hopefully, it will be enough to deal with the imp's master. He doesn't seem to be very skilled, but he's been absorbing magical energy from that creature for a very long time without giving up anything in return. It appears to have made him exceptionally strong."

"More than you know, mage," Richard said as he appeared in the doorway to the grimoire room. "I don't know how you got past my traps, but it doesn't matter. Back away from the spellbook, and I promise to make this quick."

The cretinous shopkeep raised his hands, electricity crackling between them.

"What the heck?" Theo asked. "Was I drugged?"

Richard gave a grim smile. "Nope, kid, this is real magic you're seeing. And it's too damned bad, because now I'll have to kill you too, and we happen to be in need of some fresh blood at the moment. The stronger I get, the hungrier Gaz gets, and he's just about bled Rhone dry. With all that meat on your bones, heck—you'd have kept Gaz fed for a good long while."

"You calling me fat?" Theo asked.

"Kid, if fat were a superpower, you'd be an Avenger."

"If that's the case, then you'd be Galactus," Theo countered.

Richard's face reddened for a moment, but he recovered his composure quickly. "Well, maybe so—because I do have the power cosmic. I'm not going to tell you again. Both of you, back away from the spellbook."

Crowley smiled with genuine amusement. "I don't take orders from rank amateurs, no matter how much power they've stolen—especially not one who dresses like you."

"What's wrong with the way I dress?" Richard asked.

"Not to cast aspersions on another's sartorial decisions," Crowley drily observed, "but you dress like a Skid Row bum with a cotton and flannel fetish—one who identifies as an incel and has resigned himself to a life of involuntary celibacy, forever."

"Aw, snap!" Theo said. "Geez, Richard, he just burned you like a book of matches."

"Additionally, you could stand to lose a few hundred pounds," Crowley added with a self-satisfied nod.

"Dude," Theo stage-whispered. "Fat-shaming. Totally uncool."

Crowley's brow furrowed. "This is unacceptable?"

"Absolutely," Theo replied.

"Very well. I shall resolve to avoid using such insults in the future." The wizard stared down his nose at the other man. "But he does dress like a homeless person."

"Enough!" Richard screamed, spittle flying from his lips. The slovenly magician raised his hands once more, lightning crackling from his fingertips. "This is my house, and I hand out the insults here. I was going to take it easy on you and kill you both quick, but now I'm going to make it slow and painful."

Crowley pulled the boy behind him, whispering over his shoulder. "When this starts, I want you to hide behind the grimoire's pedestal. It's protected from all sorts of magic, and he'll likely not risk damaging his own spell-book to attack you. And once you see that he's distracted, run!"

22

Honestly, Theo wasn't sure if he should trust Mr. Tall, Dark, and Mysterious. But the guy kind of reminded him of a white Denzel Washington—like Denzel from *The Equalizer*, not Denzel from *Fences*—so he figured he couldn't be all that bad. Besides that, he'd seen enough action movies to know the difference between the bad guy and the anti-hero. So as far as Theo was concerned, he'd already chosen sides.

Although he'd been unceremoniously shoved out of the way, he peeked around the man just in time to see Richard shoot lightning bolts at them, right out of his hands. Fricking lightning bolts, just like The Emperor in *Return of the Jedi*! If he hadn't been so scared, Theo would've definitely been geeking out, because it was probably the coolest thing he'd ever seen.

Or so he thought.

No sooner had Richard gone all *Revenge of the Sith* on them than the man Richard had called "mage" held his hand out and a wall of dark, shadowy mist shot out of the ground in front of him. The lightning from Richard's hands crackled and spat sparks as it danced across the mage's force shield—shadow shield?—then the spell dissipated in a cloud of smoke. And that's when things got really interesting.

In the next moment, three things happened at once. First, the mage sprouted a bunch of shadowy tentacles from his torso and back, like some sort of cross between a shadow demon and Doc Oc. Next, three of those tentacles shot out at Richard, grabbing him by the arms and legs and tossing him into the museum room. And third, a lone tentacle picked Theo up and dropped him right next to the grimoire.

"Holy crap—you're a shadow sorcerer? Please tell me you're about to summon a Hound of Ill Omen, because if you do I'm going to squee like a post-menopausal woman at a Michael Bublé concert."

The mage turned his eyes on Theo, causing the child's blood to run cold. Instead of human eyes, his eye sockets were now two bottomless pools of black emptiness that trailed away into nothing. Not only that, but his skin had gone pale, and he had streaks of black running through his skin like the Witcher when he drank a potion to buff his stats.

"Okay, I'm shitting my pants now, but this is still pretty damned cool."

"This is no game, child! A mage's dueling ground is a dangerous place to be a bystander, even for a skilled practitioner of the mystical arts. Whatever happens, do not get between us, or you will die. Instead, stick close to that pedestal and wait for your chance to flee."

"Whatever you say, Kaecilius. Now, go kick his ass—I always thought he was a dick anyway."

The mage scowled, then he took off after his opponent at speed, using those shadow limbs to walk him along several feet off the ground. Theo was scared, and that was a fact, but he was also enough of a true geek to be fascinated by what was happening. It was like real-life Dungeons & Dragons, and he was a first-level character in the midst of the inciting incident at the start of a new campaign.

"But wait—what if I'm an NPC? Aw, hell. First-level NPCs are like fodder for high-level player campaigns. Shit, I am so screwed."

Although he'd suddenly become acutely aware of just how much danger he was in, the boy still couldn't resist sneaking over to the doorway to watch the battle. And what a battle it was. Richard's repertoire seemed to be limited to elemental magic—fireballs, lightning bolts, ice spikes, and the like, which he kept spamming at his opponent without letting up. It was completely uninspired, in Theo's opinion, but effective because he seemed to be a bit OP.

On the other hand, watching the mage work was like seeing a master artist at his craft. He kept picking off Richard's attacks with his many shadowy tentacles, while counterattacking by lashing the other magician with the same, or striking him with shadow bolts, or confusing him by disappearing in a cloud of shadow only to reappear in another place.

The strangest thing was that they were crashing into and through the displays without damaging a single one. Sure, they knocked a few over, but the glass didn't break or even show a single crack. It was bizarre, but Theo was more concerned with the outcome of the fight than he was with figuring out why they weren't breaking the scenery.

After the duel had gone on for a few minutes, Richard seemed to be gaining strength while the mage appeared to be slowing down. At first, he was able to keep up with the shopkeeper's attacks, creating shields for protection against fireballs and lightning bolts and knocking the ice spikes and flaming meteors out of the air before they reached him. But then he misjudged the timing of his defense, and a flaming rock hit him in the shoulder.

The mage spun, grasping his injury as he fell to his knees. He recovered quickly, sending a salvo of shadow bolts at the fat magician, but Richard simply batted them away with flaming hands as he advanced on his now-wounded prey. Then, the mage growled, his eyes spewing trailing tendrils of shadow as he sprung a multitude of shadow tentacles from his body, each one snapping out to wrap the fat-assed magician up like thick strands of spider-silk.

At that moment, Theo was certain his new ally would be victorious. Each strand of smoke and shadow seemed to tighten around the fat man by the second, causing his face to redden as they slowly constricted him to death. But that was not to be the end of Richard. The corpulent comic book store owner screamed, flexing his arms as well as his prodigious belly, snapping the dark restraints all at once.

As he did, the mage's shadow limbs seemed to thin and falter. Then, they dissipated into mist as the tall dark stranger stumbled to the floor.

23

C rowley couldn't believe how much magical energy the fat magician had at his disposal. He'd fought and won many such duels before, even against fae sorcerers who had ample access to Underhill's magic. This had been due to the fact that even a skilled mage had limits regarding how much power they could channel.

But this inferior, unskilled buffoon had spent years saving up magic and storing it in his massive, overweight body, and what he lacked in talent he made up for in sheer, raw power. He was a living magic battery, a human power sink for mystical potential. Therefore, he didn't have to channel any energy, because it was already inside of him. How Crowley had failed to sense the man's enormous mystical reserves was a question for another time, but one he would surely revisit—should he manage to survive this encounter.

Now, the shadow mage was spent, his own magical reserves nearly run dry. He could give himself over to other internal forces that were available, but that would result in a devil's bargain that he might regret for all eternity. At least the child was safe, small comfort that might be.

Crowley raised his head to look his opponent in the eye as the boorish, overpowered imbecile grabbed him by the throat with a flaming hand. Richard lifted him in the air effortlessly, holding him aloft with strength derived from mystical forces that he had not earned nor even mastered. But it had been more than enough to stymy Crowley's efforts to defeat him. The power gained from sacrificing young, innocent souls was nothing to scoff at.

The shopkeep eyed him with a gleam in his eye, his flaccid lips nibbling at a crumb in his beard as he did. "You were tough, I'll give you that. And that shadow magic—wow! If I didn't think you'd turn on me at the first opportunity, I'd keep you as a slave and make you teach me that stuff. But I can't risk it. So, any last words?"

Crowley spat in his eye.

Theo could hardly believe what he was seeing. The dark, mysterious mage was about to get his neck snapped by that fat human shit-stain, Richard. Not that Theo had room to talk about being overweight—he could stand to lose a few pounds himself.

But as Theo saw it, being out of shape was a personal choice that hurt no one. On the other hand, being a total dick and treating the people around you like shit? *That* was totally uncalled for, and Richard absolutely pushed the envelope when it came to insensitivity and cruelty toward others.

As he watched Richard squeezing the life out of the mage, Theo realized that the comic store owner was just another bully, another person who lorded his position, popularity, and power over others just to feel good about himself.

The mage was kind of an asshole too, but he at least seemed to be working on it. A real asshole wouldn't have stuck his neck out for some dumb kid. So, Theo wasn't going to let him die, not if he could help it.

He looked around for a way to help the mage, but all he saw were swords and axes and stuff like that. Theo wasn't a fighter, and he had no idea how to crank a cross-bow, much less aim one. Heck, he'd be more likely to kill the mage than put a bolt between Richard's beady little eyes.

And even if he did, he doubted it would hurt him—not after all the punishment he'd absorbed during his battle with the mage. If he could take that, a crossbow bolt wouldn't do much more than tickle him.

So, how was Theo going to make a difference?

He glanced around one more time, then it hit him—the spellbook. If Richard's power came from the ledork, then maybe Theo could cast a spell to cut him off from the source. It was worth a shot.

The boy dashed over to the grimoire and began to read aloud. The words were strangely written, and he stumbled over their pronunciation at first. But as he read, the spelling became clearer, as if the book were adapting to his speech patterns. Theo then started over again, reading the entire spell in a single breath.

When he finished, it was like everything froze for an instant, like time had been captured on the surface of a bubble that was just about to burst. Then there was a pop —not an audible one, but something he felt down in his soul, a release of energy that made him dizzy and a little bit nauseous as well.

At that moment, he caught the sound of laughter coming from the reading room, soon to be drowned out by Richard's wailing cry.

"Noooooo! What have you done?"

Theo stumbled to the museum room doorway, breathing hard from the exertion as he reached the threshold. He felt like he'd run a marathon, and he leaned heavily against the doorway as he watched events unfold between the two magic-users. As the boy looked on, the tall, dark stranger slipped from Richard's grasp, landing somewhat unsteadily on his feet as his opponent stumbled to his knees.

"Please don't kill me," Richard begged. "If you want the spellbook, you can take it—I'll find another. You want gold? I have plenty of that, and bearer bonds, e-currency, you name it. I'll even let you take Gaz. I mean, he's just going to kill me now anyway."

The man stared down at Richard with cold eyes. "It's not what I want from you, it's what *it* wants. And it is very, very hungry."

A shadow rose up from the tall man's shoulders like a cobra's mantle, high above him until it scraped the ceiling.

The darkness then broke like a wave over Richard, enveloping him as it consumed the store owner from the inside out, until nothing was left but an empty, dried husk.

Theo would hear Richard's screams in his nightmares for years to come.

24

Crowley sat with the boy in a back room of the comic book shop, thumbing through the comics he'd taken as the boy did the same with his own stack. Once the illusions fell, the child's only concerns had been whether Richard actually had any rare editions of collectible comic books, and what would become of them.

Theo had momentarily forgotten about the older teen, so enrapt was he with the events that had occurred during Crowley's battle with Richard. That was just as well, as Gaz had finished the youth off as soon as he was freed of his bond with Richard. The shadow wizard would have to concoct a suitable lie to assuage the boy's guilt, should he start asking after Rhone—and he'd have to deal with the lidérc as well.

But one thing at a time. The creature had been contained, and while Theo was unaware, he was now bonded with the imp. Crowley knew how to rid him of it, but for now he thought it best to keep their bond a secret, until the boy was of sufficient age to decide how he wished to deal with it. Until then, it would remain hidden safely away in the basement, where the shadow wizard could keep an eye on it.

And, of course, there was the matter of the boy's affinity for magic.

"Can I keep the grimoire? I promise I'll only look at it. I won't even cast any more spells."

The shadow mage frowned. "I told you more than once already, the answer is no. Now, it's time for you to leave. There will be some very nasty people along shortly who will be very concerned about a young, seemingly mundane child who witnessed a duel between two powerful magicians. If you wish to retain your memories of the last week, and also to avoid potentially suffering permanent and irreversible brain damage, I suggest you take your comics and run on home."

"Man, you're no fun."

"So I've been told. If you wish to keep yourself and your family safe, I strongly advise you to avoid speaking of what you've seen with anyone—not even your closest friend."

Theo stared down at his comics, running a finger across the cover of *Moon Knight* #1. "If I do, will you eat me like you did Richard?"

Crowley paused. He considered his next words quite carefully, as it was a sensitive topic for all involved.

"No, because despite my admittedly unpleasant disposition, I'm not the type to feed young boys to creatures from the shadow dimension." He leaned forward, lifting the child's chin with a long, scarred finger. "However, if you reveal my secret to anyone, there will be dire consequences. Am I understood?"

The boy nodded, eyes wide. "STEM Scout's honor, I won't tell a soul."

Crowley considered him for what was most certainly an unbearably long time for the child. "Indeed, it would be best that you didn't."

Theo gulped.

"Now, gather your things. It's time for you to go." The shadow wizard watched the boy in silence as he packed his booty in his backpack. "Oh, and Theo? Stay away from the comic book shop for a few days, then resume your usual routine. And if you should see someone who looks like Richard at the front counter, treat them as such. But do not, under any circumstances, accompany them anywhere alone, no matter what they promise you."

Theo double gulped. "Yes, sir."

"That's a good child. Now run along."

The boy scrambled out the door just as fast as his stumpy little legs would carry him. Crowley walked to the door, considering the possibilities as the chubby youth disappeared around the corner. He would need to take on an apprentice, eventually—and the boy did show promise.

But that could wait. At the moment, Crowley had to find a doppelgänger on short notice, and deal with Maeve's fixers to boot. He sighed, rubbing his temples, then he locked the door. Thankfully, the lidérc would know where the gold was hidden and the bodies buried.

Thus, from the shadow mage's point of view, the day was already starting to look up.

AUTHOR'S NOTE

The events of this short story occur just after Book 9 in the Colin McCool Paranormal Suspense Series. To avoid spoilers, make sure you've read *Druid Apprentice* before you jump into this story.

BREAKING UP IS HARD TO DO

In which Colin helps Larry the Chupacabra break up with his ex...

25

The trail led us to a dark, narrow lane behind a popular upscale bar, just a block over from the city's famed 6th Street district. Trash and other less sanitary detritus littered the pavement, and the air carried the scents of vomit, human urine, rotting garbage, and stale beer. There might have been worse ways to spend my last 72 hours in Austin than hunting down a zombie corgi, but at the moment I couldn't think of any.

"Larry, do you have her scent or not?"

The scraggly chupacabra kept his nose to the pavement as he replied. "Keep your panties on, druid," he said in a thick Brooklyn accent. "I'm workin' on it."

"Well, hurry the hell up. I'm freezing my ass off, it's late, and there are some very bad people looking for me. The last thing I need is to be cornered in a dark alley by Aenghus or one of his cronies."

"Like I told ya', if you'd stop killing gods, they'd stop wanting to revenge murder you."

"Dermot was a demigod," I countered. "And I killed Kulkulkan's avatar, not the god itself."

"Same diff," Larry said as he sniffed a suspicious-looking puddle. He took an experimental lick, wrinkling his snout before continuing. "You kill their offspring, they go all 'eye for an eye' and stuff. Seems like simple math to me."

"They're coming after me because they see me as a threat, not because—" I paused mid-sentence, pinching the bridge of my nose. "Ah, forget it. Just focus on finding your ex and let me worry about which gods are hunting me and why."

"Sure, whatever you say," Larry replied sardonically.

My tragically ugly companion continued down the dark alleyway, sniffing the pavement and stopping at random intervals to examine whatever captured his interest. At first, I'd thought he was sussing out a spoor trail that would lead us to the pint-sized, undead rat killer who currently stalked the streets of downtown Austin. But after Larry gobbled down a half-eaten order of street tacos, I began to suspect that catching his ex was not exactly his highest priority.

As the mangy, bald canid dug through a pile of trash that had spilled out of a restaurant's dumpster, I noticed movement in the shadows down the alley.

"Um, Larry?"

"Hold on a sec, I'm kinda busy here," he replied as he continued to root through the garbage.

"Larry, there's something coming our way, and I don't think it's friendly."

"You're a druid. Use your magic whatchamacallits to scare it off."

"My 'whatchamacallits'?"

"Yeah, don't you have a magic wand or somethin'? Just *expelliarmus* the thing, or whatever you wizard-types do."

The ominous shadows at the end of the alley spread in a slow, inexorable march toward us. Instinctively I took a step back, but Larry remained oblivious to the danger. The chupacabra crouched on his forepaws with his snout deep inside an over-flowing garbage bag, ass in the air without a care in the world. I shook my head at the cryptid as my ears picked up the faint *click-click-click* of tiny claws skittering across concrete.

That can't be good.

Muttering a trigger word in Gaelic, I cast a night-vision cantrip so I could see what the hell we were dealing with... because it sure wasn't a damned zombie corgi.

Shit fuck shit!

"We got company!" I yelled as I backed away from the rapidly-spreading shadows.

Larry pulled his head out of the trash bag, spinning around with a growl. "Damn it, druid, how do you expect me to work in these conditions? I mean, I don't go to your junkyard and tell you to deal with customers while you're wrenching on some old heap."

"Larry, look behind you—slowly," I whispered as my fingers danced through a series of intricate, arcane gestures.

The rat-like dog creature puffed out his bony chest. "Do I look stupid? Wait, don't answer that. Say, did you know that your hands are glowing? Might wanna get that checked out—it looks pretty serious."

My magic pushed back the darkness as actinic sparks danced between my fingers. With both eyes glued to the alley beyond, I pointed a glowing digit over my companion's shoulder. "Don't make any sudden moves, and when I say duck—"

The chupacabra whipped his head around and froze as the light from my hands glittered off hundreds of pairs of tiny red eyes. Finally recognizing the danger, he gulped and froze.

"Is that—?"

I nodded. "Yup. Your ex's victims, apparently."

"What should I do?" he whispered.

"Duck!" I yelled as I cut loose with lightning bolts from both hands, strafing the narrow passage with electricity while quickly backpedaling from the mass of undead rodents that now streamed toward us. As my spell made contact, dozens of little zombie rat bodies cooked from the inside out, popping like eggs in a microwave. Meanwhile, Larry disappeared, presumably to make his escape while leaving me behind as a convenient distraction.

What's that old joke about surviving the zombie apocalypse? 'You only have to run faster than the next guy?' Thanks, Larry.

Backing out of the alley and onto 7th Street, I sized up the situation as my lightning spell petered out. Norway rats were pretty damned fast, and from the looks of it, being recently deceased hadn't slowed them down. My spell had certainly cut a swathe through their ranks, but due to their sheer numbers, it had done little to deter the mass of rodents that now flowed forth in a river of decaying rodent flesh from the alley.

Much to my chagrin, there was no shortage of pedestrians and cars on the streets and sidewalks of downtown Austin this night. The crowd was a mix of young professionals, college students, and homeless people panhandling for their next meal or fix. Little did they know they were about to be overrun by a mischief of zombie rats.

Being no stranger to aggressive rodents, the homeless were the first to scatter as the rat swarm flooded out of the alley. But like most people in modern society, the rest of the crowd remained blissfully oblivious to the encroaching danger, and would likely remain so until it was much too late. With a sigh, I drew my Glock and fired three shots in the air.

"Fly, you fools!" I shouted at the people milling about.

Overkill? Not really. A plague of undead Norwegian rats wasn't nearly as intimidating as a balrog, but the little fuckers could be just as deadly. It'd only take one person getting bit, and we'd be facing last year's undead outbreak all over again.

Snickering to myself at the tangentially apropos Tolkien reference, I tossed the Glock in my Craneskin Bag. The last thing I needed was to be holding a gun when the cops showed up, and since I was the only person who could access it, the pocket dimension inside the Bag provided a convenient place to ditch the weapon.

Now, to deal with these rats.

By the time I'd gotten rid of the pistol, the crowd had scattered—random gunfire will do that to people these days. The rats remained fixated on me, chasing me farther into the street as cars swerved past, horns blaring. Since police headquarters was right down the street, I estimated that I had about a minute until APD showed up looking to make an arrest.

I did love a good challenge, and the fact that I couldn't shift made the situation that much more interesting. Despite the bad mood I'd been in earlier, a broad grin split my face as I cracked my neck and bounced on my toes in the middle of the street.

Time to work.

26

First on the agenda was to make sure nobody got in the line of fire, and that I didn't get run over trying to take these little fuckers out of commission.

Time to try out some of the new spells Finnegas has been showing me.

I thrust my arms out left and right, fingers up and palms extended as if pushing against two invisible walls.

Here goes nothing.

"*Balla lasair!*" I shouted, channeling magical energy out of my arms and into the street, aiming about twenty feet away on either side of me. Fire gushed from my open palms, and where it hit the pavement, a wall of flame shot up twenty feet high and ten feet deep. I swept the gouts of fire back and forth across the street and sidewalks, sealing the immediate area off with a flame barrier that ran from the buildings on one side of the street to the other.

That oughta keep the traffic and bystanders away, and keep the rats from escaping. Johnny Storm, eat your heart out.

No sooner had I cast my firewall spell than I felt something crawling up my jeans. Instinctively, I screamed like a little girl as I kicked a six-inch-long undead rodent off me, causing it to sail into the wall of fire and burst into flame. A quick glance around told me it was a loner—but the rest weren't far behind.

"Nicely done there, Jonah Hill," a disembodied voice quipped from somewhere behind me. "Private Wilhelm's got nothing on you."

"Fuck you very much, Larry," I replied, feigning nonchalance as I quickly checked my leg for bites. "Undead people I can deal with. But undead animals? That's a whole lot of nope for me."

"Hey, now!" he protested. "I dated one and she wasn't so bad."

"Not so bad? Have you forgotten that Kiki tried to turn you into a zombie? And need I remind you she's the reason we're being attacked by a zombie rat swarm?"

"Speak for yourself—from where I'm sitting, they're after you. And besides, I did my part by finding her minions, didn't I? My work is done, my friend. Now I'm just over here enjoying the show."

"Thanks, you're a real pal," I replied, scowling as my eyes swept back to the mass of zombie rats rolling toward me. There were hundreds on the street now, and possibly thousands behind them. From the looks of it, the zombie vyrus had spread rapidly through Austin's rat population after Larry's ex began feeding on them.

Seems like a pretty rapid rate of transmission for standard zombism. And where have I seen that before? The Dark Druid engineered a more contagious form of the vyrus not long ago, but he's out of commission. Definitely something to look into, after I deal with this infestation.

The skittering of thousands of little claws on concrete brought my thoughts back to the present. Fearing I'd be overrun, I ran to the other side of the street and scrambled into the bed of a lifted Ford 4x4, knowing it would only buy me a few seconds at best. Rats could climb like no one's business, and despite my high perch, they'd be running over the sides of the truck's bed in short order.

If only I could get all the rats in one place—then I could incinerate them with my flame wall spell.

The trick would be getting them bunched up so I could take them out in one fell swoop. Right now, they were crowding around the car, and I'd trap myself if I lit them up. No bueno. What I needed was a way to immobilize them so I could get some distance and then burn them to ash and dust. For that, I was pretty sure I had just the thing.

Mogh's Scythe should do nicely.

In Irish mythology, Mogh Roith was a famous battle druid known for selling his services to the highest bidder. When King Cormac mac Airt decided to raid Munster—based on bad advice from the fae, go figure—old Mogh singlehandedly ran off his entire army, defeating all Cormac's druids as well. According to my mentor Finnegas, Mogh was one bad dude, and possibly the most powerful battlemage to ever cast a spell on Irish soil.

Heh—my kind of druid.

One of the spells Mogh created was this badass conjuration known as Mogh's Scythe. Ingeniously simple in its design but rather difficult to cast, the spell consisted of nothing more than a thin sheet of super-compressed air traveling at high speed toward one's enemies. It didn't seem like much in theory, but in practice, it was like shooting giant razor blades across a battlefield.

I'd just started learning the spell, and thus far I couldn't cut more than a few small sticks in half with it. But rat legs weren't much thicker than twigs, so I figured it'd be just the thing for dealing with ye olde rat swarm. But, as I said, it was a rather difficult casting. The blood-thirsty little fuckers were already piling on top of each other in an attempt to get at me, so I had precious little time to work.

Better hop to it.

The act of compressing air molecules with magic was no mean feat, and against my better judgment, I closed my eyes to cast the spell. In order to make it work, the caster had to super-compress a vast volume of gases—and that was just the first part of the spell. Then, you had to send the air mass out in a specific direction with sufficient velocity to cause injury, all while maintaining mental control over the air molecules so your spell didn't dissipate before it hit the target.

And I had to do it before thousands of disease-carrying undead rats swarmed my pale ginger ass.

No pressure, Colin, old boy. No pressure at all.

27

In theory, a magus should be able to cast a spell without trigger words, arcane gestures, or spell ingredients. But because magic was, at its essence, a highly conceptual practice, such devices made it easier for spellcasters to focus their magic. That's why some magic-users —witches being the prime example—required actual physical components to cast their spells. We druids did not, because we relied on our close connection with nature to power and control our magic.

However, it was impossible to maintain individual control over millions upon millions of air molecules at the same time—thus, visualization was the key to casting Mogh's Scythe. In fact, when casting any sort of druid magic, intent and will were much more important than mechanics. We druids channeled our intentions by visualizing what we wanted our magic to do, then we manifested our spells with sheer willpower and an innate affinity for nature's workings.

"Ya' better hurry, druid, or them rats are gonna be havin' you for a midnight snack!"

Ignoring Larry's warning and the sound of the rat swarm approaching, I focused on casting the spell. The first step was creating a mental image of two huge hands compressing a hundred-foot column of air in front of the truck. In my mind, I pictured the air being trapped inside those huge hands, building tremendous pressure to be released at my command.

And indeed, air rushed past me to fill the vacuum created as I initiated the spell. It was a good sign, but while practicing in the Grove under Finnegas' supervision, I'd had difficulty compressing a sufficient volume of gas to power the casting. I could only hope I'd trapped enough air to create the effect I desired.

Time to find out.

"*Gearradh trí rud!*" I exclaimed, opening my eyes as I triggered the spell.

My druid sight allowed me to observe the effects of the spell in real-time. In the magical spectrum, it looked like a luminescent sheet of glass expanding outward from the focal point of the spell. For a moment, the asphalt and concrete took on an iridescent sheen that traveled from the truck to the cars and buildings opposite in a split-second. The rat swarm instantly stopped its march toward me as tens of thousands of tiny undead rat feet were severed.

There was a moment's silence, then all those undead rats began to squeal and cry in unison. At the same moment, the tires blew out on every car parked along the other side of the street. A second later, a fire hydrant flew into the sky, powered by a torrent of water that quickly flooded the sidewalk and road.

"Well, that was unexpected—and kinda fucked up," I muttered, suddenly realizing that the busted fire hydrant posed two very real and troubling challenges to my plan.

For starters, a large portion of Lieutenant Dan's undead rat swarm was now in danger of being washed into the sewer. Like human zombies, they tended to move in herds when they gathered in large numbers. We'd lucked out by stumbling over their swarm, since it had given me the opportunity to take them all out at once. However, if even one rat got away, it might still bite another animal or human and start a whole new zombie outbreak.

To add insult to injury, the water blowing out of the hydrant had rapidly soaked the zombie rats, making it very, very difficult to incinerate them.

Hmm... then again, maybe I don't have to.

"Larry, find someplace to hide."

"Why? They can't see me, and even if they could I can run faster than—"

"Now, Larry!"

"Okay, sheesh," he grumbled, cursing me under his breath as his disembodied voice drifted away.

A few rats were already floating toward the sewer drain, carried by the torrent of water shooting out of the decapitated fire hydrant. As my eyes glanced over the errant hydrant that lay in the street, I noticed that it had been cleanly shorn off at the base. Later, I'd puzzle out how I'd been suddenly able to channel so much power into that spell—after I dealt with more immediate concerns.

I turned my attention back to the rats, creating a clear image in my mind of what I intended to do. They may have been soaked and therefore resistant to incineration, but they were by no means immune to heat energy. And as for what I was about to do, well—Maeve's people would just have to clean it up.

As I readied the firewall spell a second time, I pointed my open palms not at the rats, but at the growing puddle of water that surrounded them. Shouting the trigger words for the spell once more, I concentrated all the heat and flame into the water, forcing the water molecules to absorb the entirety of the energy from the release of magic. Hundreds of gallons of water boiled into steam, cooking every last rat like a mudbug at a cajun crawfish boil.

The stench that resulted was immediate and horrendous. Instantly, the rodents' skin and flesh deliquesced, creating a putrid, steaming hot stew of dead rat meat, fur, and bones in the middle of one of Austin's busiest streets. After spending months fighting the undead in the Hellpocalypse, I'd certainly dealt with worse... but not by much. At the rate water was pumping out of that hydrant, it'd soon wash down into the sewers—but the smell would likely last for days.

I shrugged. *Not my problem.*

Carefully, oh so carefully, I climbed off the back of the truck to search for any rats that might have escaped. After finding none—and retching every few steps—I took a moment to survey the full scope of the carnage. Soon, a giggle bubbled up from that juvenile part of me where my inner ten-year-old remained. Before I knew it, I found myself in a full-on fit of uncontrollable laughter.

After my laughing attack passed, I pulled out my phone and snapped a picture of the slaughter. In a brief flash of inspiration, I quickly texted it to the contact number I had for Maeve's bootlickers, content in the knowledge that the local faery queen wouldn't find it half as amusing as I did. Sirens sounded in the distance as I tucked my phone away, signaling that it was time to go. As I contacted the Druid Oak to portal me home, I couldn't help but crack a smile as I commented on my own work.

"Rats—boiled again."

28

E ven after all this time, portalling back to the Druid Oak was still pretty weird. Shaking off the latent dizziness and general muzzy-headed feeling it gave me, I rubbed my tired eyes and made a beeline for the hot springs.

Until recently I'd been bathing in the cool, clear waters of the Grove's creek. Then one day Finnegas came along and calmly asked me why I was still taking baths in cold water, when the Grove could easily create a heated, spring-fed pool for me. After kicking myself in the ass a few times, I asked the Grove to take care of it. Since then, I'd been using the damned thing several times a week.

Privacy was rarely an issue inside the Druid Grove, because the Oak only allowed a few select individuals to enter. As the master of the Grove, obviously I was tops on that list. Besides me, only Finnegas and Maureen could come and go as they pleased here; everyone else had to be ferried in by me personally, or brought here by the Oak on request. Since the old man and the half-kelpie were busy getting our affairs together Earthside, I had the place to myself.

Assured I would not be disturbed, I began to strip off my clothes on my way to the springs, starting with kicking off my boots and peeling my nasty socks from my feet. I'd gotten my feet wet while boiling the zombie rats, so the sooner I could get barefoot, the better. The boots would be cleaned by the Grove—microbes and all that—but the socks were a lost cause, so I sent a mental message to the Grove to recycle them.

From there, I sniffed my jacket and shirt, only to find that both smelled of boiled zombies. I peeled those off as well, hoping like hell that a good wash in the creek could get the smell out. The t-shirt was easily replaced, but the jacket was an expensive level IIIA bulletproof flight jacket that Maureen had purchased from a supplier in Israel. Apparently she'd ordered it right before I learned to control my *ríastrad*, and she'd promptly dug it out of storage after my fight with Diarmuid, insisting that I wear it.

I sent a mental image of the dirty jacket, Maureen's angry face, the jacket clean, and Maureen smiling at the Grove, and received an image of a sunny day in reply. Translation? "No problem, I got this." I thanked my lucky stars for being a druid with a magical, sentient, pocket dimension at my disposal and began stripping out of my jeans.

"Heya, druid," a familiar and disembodied voice said from right behind me, just as I was about to free my left leg. Startled, I lost my balance and fell on my ass with my jeans tangled around my ankles.

"Larry? Fucking hell, how'd you get in here?"

"How'd ya' think? I followed you here, is how."

"You mean the Oak brought you?" I asked.

"Naw, I just walked right in when you called for your druid Uber."

"That's impossible," I replied. "The Oak doesn't just let people—or chupacabras—walk in unannounced."

I could hear the shrug in Larry's voice as he replied. "Meh, whatever. I'm gonna stay invisible though, if you don't mind. I get the feeling this place doesn't like me very much."

Larry's presence puzzled the shit out of me, but I decided to chalk it up to the fact that the chupacabra was anything but your typical supernatural creature. According to him, he was a hodgepodge of various natural and magical beings, cooked up in a government lab on Plum Island for who knew what purpose. Larry claimed they'd been trying to create battle Wargs, but from the look of him, I doubted very seriously that was his makers' intent when they created him.

"You think?" I said as I struggled to get my pants back on. "Don't take it personally, Larry. The Grove is very orthodox when it comes to the natural order. Gene-splicing and other forms of genetic tampering rub it the wrong way."

"Hmph, like it has the right to point its branches at me. I don't know if you're aware, but your Grove is a flippin' amalgam of nature, deific magic, and a lot of other stuff that I still haven't figured out."

I considered Larry's words for a moment, quickly concluding that his observations were probably right on the money. The Dagda had gifted me with a magical acorn that had grown into the Druid Oak when I planted it in the junkyard. After what I'd seen since that fateful day, I was positive that he and Goibniu, and possibly Lugh as well, had used massive amounts of magic to create it.

Both the Oak and Grove possessed god-like powers that dwarfed those of any mage, human and fae included. That alone made the nature of its creation suspect. You didn't get a magical plane-hopping, pocket-dimension-creating, sentient tree by leaving its DNA alone, that was for sure.

"Larry, I'd be the last person to argue that point with you. But what I really want to know is, why are you here instead of tracking down your ex?"

"Right. Well, there's something you need to know about Kiki."

I bit back a sigh. "Okay... but can't it wait until I have a bath and take a nap? Time moves so slowly here, and Kiki will still be there when I'm done."

"This is important, druid. Trust me, I wouldn't have risked coming here and pissing off your magic mutant tree if it wasn't."

Something told me this would take a while, so I grabbed my shirt and started pulling it back on. "Why do I get the feeling I'm going to regret what you're about to tell me?"

"Yeah, well—I probably shoulda' told you, and I meant to, but—"

"But the timing wasn't right, the stars weren't in alignment, and Nostradamus hadn't written a stanza mentioning what you should've told me. Does that about sum it up?"

"Geez, druid. If I knew you was going to be an ass about it—"

"Oh, please. Don't act all wounded," I said with sarcasm in my voice. "Now, tell me what you came to say."

Larry was still invisible, but I could hear him scratching nervously nearby. "You see, druid, it's like this. You know how I told you Kiki is a zombie corgi and all that?"

"Yes."

"Well, she's actually more than that. Like, a lot more."

"A lot more, how?"

Larry scratched some more before he answered, a nervous tell if there ever was one. "She's... I mean to say Kiki is... er, what I'm trying to say is that—"

"Cripes' sakes, Larry, I'm not getting any younger. Spit it out already."

The chupacabra sighed loudly. "Alright, it's like this. Kiki is a—"

At that moment, the air directly in front of me spun into a vortex that stretched away into the distance—a long, narrow tunnel made up of wind, dirt, grass, and leaves. And Larry, who I was able to see because he displaced so much of the detritus that got sucked into the vortex. In less than a second, the chupacabra's shimmering outline had disappeared from sight, and the disturbance dissipated as if it had never been there.

Like a turd in the wind, the Grove had just flushed Larry from its system.

29

"Damn it!" I hissed under my breath. "Okay, where did you send him?"

The Grove sent me an image of a stallion shaking horse shit from its hoof, followed by another image of the junkyard, adjacent to the Druid Oak's spot.

"Send me there, please, if you don't mind."

The sentient pocket dimension sent me another image, one that was me, but not me. This me had pale, gray-green skin, black teeth, chapped lips, and torn, peeling flesh that oozed maggots and pus.

Well—I could've gone my whole life without seeing that and never lost a night of sleep. I will now, though.

Although the Grove didn't know it—because no one did, except for Fallyn—I'd had nightmares for months after coming back from the Hellpocalypse. Once I'd readjusted to life in this timeline, they'd slowly faded away. But there wasn't a day that went by when I didn't think about

Anna, Mickey, and the group of kids I'd left behind in that other, post-apocalyptic timeline.

Click had assured me that eventually I'd be able to go back to the exact time and place he'd yanked me out of in that world. Even so, it still felt like I had abandoned them. Months later, I occasionally woke up screaming with visions of undead children in my head.

Enough of that—focus on the now, Colin.

"Look, I know you don't like Larry. But he has his uses, and right now I need him to stop an undead outbreak from happening."

Which apparently is a weekly occurrence in Austin these days.

The Grove sent another image, this one of me being pulled down under a horde of deaders.

"Yes, it's dangerous, but it's also my job. Nobody else gives a shit. The factions are too caught up in their own affairs, and they're each way too insular to give a damn about what happens to the humans on a day-to-day basis. Let's face it, they prefer to clean up after a disaster happens rather than bothering to avert a crisis beforehand. And with the Cold Iron Circle gone to ground, it falls to me to avert shit like this."

Which brought up an interesting question—what was going to happen to the city after I was gone? Seriously, it made me wonder who'd taken care of stuff like this before I came on the scene.

Certainly the Circle had done their part, if only out of self-preservation and self-interest, and the city had a healthy population of freelance hunters. But would it be enough? Sometimes, I couldn't help but think that things had been a lot quieter on the supernatural front before I'd gotten clued into The World Beneath.

World-class shit magnet—that's me, alright. Speaking of which, I still need to find out what Larry was going to tell me.

The Grove sent a few more images of me in dire straits, until I'd finally had enough. "Look, would you cut it out already? Just send me where Larry is and stop worrying about me so much. I can take care of myself."

With those words, my pet pocket dimension went radio-silent. A split-second later, I found myself standing in the junkyard, right next to Roscoe and Rufus. The two dobie-bully mixes were jumping up and down as they barked at something hidden atop a stack of crushed cars. The dogs howled and growled, never taking their eyes off their invisible prey, like a couple of hounds treeing a mountain lion.

"Roscoe, Rufus, hush!" I said in a calm but firm voice. Immediately, the two sat on their haunches, tongues lolling with their eyes still focused at the top of the stack. "Good boys. Okay, I got this—you guys go find Finnegas and bug him for a treat."

As soon as they heard "Finnegas" and "treat," the pair took off at a run. Back when Finn was still hooked on heroin and living in the junkyard, the pups had discovered he was a sucker for puppy dog eyes and an expertly-timed whine. That probably had a lot to do with the fact that the dogs didn't judge him for being a junkie, and thus they'd been his only companions for a time. The old man still spoiled them, and it was rare that he didn't have a dog biscuit or liver treat at hand these days.

When the dogs were gone, I cupped my hands to shout at the top of the stack of cars. "You can come down now, Larry—they're gone."

A disembodied, nearly hairless, rat-like dog's head shimmered into view fifteen feet above me. "You sure?"

"Positive. Now, come down and finish what you were telling me back in the Grove."

Larry's head slowly swiveled back and forth as he verified my claim. "Nope, no can do. As soon as those mutts scarf down a Scooby snack, they'll be right back here giving me grief. Meet me in the parking lot and I'll tell you what's up."

"Arrgh! Fine, I'll be there in a second."

A minute later, I was standing outside the front gate, waiting for the chupacabra to come into view. Say what you would about Larry—he was a survivor. And that meant he was smart enough to avoid popping into view out in the open, because the last thing he wanted was to draw attention. Soon, he came trotting out from behind a customer's car looking like a cross between a mangy coyote and a large, hairless Chihuahua.

"Let's take a walk, druid," he said as he loped off toward the street.

Cursing under my breath, I paused for a second before following. All impatience aside, it'd be easier to talk with him away from the junkyard anyway. No matter how hippyish Austin was, folks still gave the side-eye to people who had full-blown conversations with stray dogs, after all.

Soon we were walking down South Congress, just another a college kid taking his pound pup for a walk. After twenty steps or so, I cleared my throat imploringly.

"You sick or somethin'? Sounds like you're comin' down with a cold."

"Quit being a smartass and tell me what the deal is with Kiki."

"Sheesh, who pissed in your cornflakes this morning? It's not like this is easy for me to talk about, you know."

"Larry..." I said threateningly.

"Alright, alright—I can take a hint." He loped ahead a few steps, stopping and tilting his head as he looked up at me. "You know how you kicked that necromancer's ass back at Big Bend?"

"Yes, Larry, I remember it well. Seeing how I almost died and all. What's that have to do with Kiki? Did the Dark Druid create her or something?"

"Um, sort of. But it's worse than that."

I scratched my head and scowled. "Worse than—? Aw, hell—just spit it out, already."

"Ya' see, it's like this... Kiki learned necromancy from that Darkwing Druid prick."

30

"Say what? Whoa, now, back up. How's a freaking zombified corgi learn necromancy from an evil, semi-immortal druid?"

"Ya' see, that's just the thing—she ain't no normal corgi."

I knuckled my forehead, because I had a headache coming on. "Well, duh—she's a freaking zombie, Larry."

The chupacabra absently scratched at his neck with his hind paw. "Sure, there's that. But the kicker is that she wasn't always a corgi. Kiki used to be human."

I covered my eyes with my hand and exhaled, counting to ten in my mind. "You're fucking with me, right?"

"Would I bullshit a bullshitter? No, I'm not kidding. Sheesh, did you think I was slapping cheeks with a freaking dog? I got better taste than that. And besides, what would we talk about?"

"Okay, that bit of imagery is now burned into my

memory for all time, so thanks for that. Now, you mind telling me how this happened?"

"Oh, you know how it goes. A devastatingly handsome and utterly dashing chupacabra meets an undead corgi with an ass that just won't quit, they have a few drinks, and then bam! Romance strikes. How was I supposed to know she was a complete nutcase?"

"First off, the fact that she was a human trapped inside a zombie corgi's body should have been your first clue. And second, I wasn't asking about how you hooked up with her. I want to know how in the hell a human's consciousness ended up inside an undead animal."

"Oh, that." Larry belched loudly. "Sorry, this whole thing with my ex is giving me gas like you wouldn't believe. Anyhow, Kiki was some sort of hedge witch or something a hundred years ago, or thereabouts. She met your former nemesis, the two had a fling—what she saw in that douchebag, who can say—and he taught her some necromancy. Although, I think he mixed up the spells or something, just to be a dick."

Just then, a car full of teens passed us by as the driver laid on the horn. A round-faced guy about my age leaned out the rear window, beer can in hand as he hollered at me. "Get a job, you fucking freak!"

I flipped him off without looking, chewing my lip as I considered Larry's story. "Wouldn't surprise me if he did. The Fear Doirich was a druid to the Tuatha De Danann. In his mind, he's a god—and the gods love nothing more than playing nasty tricks on mortals. Especially when they think they're getting uppity, grasping for things like deific levels of power and immortality."

"Yeah, exactly. So anyway, the dick up and leaves her one day, and Kiki starts blaming herself. Checking herself in the mirror looking for wrinkles, cellulite, that sort of thing. Pretty soon, she decides he split because she was getting long in the tooth, and she hatches a plan to turn the clock back."

Tires squealed in the distance. I glanced up, noting that the car full of college kids was turning around. Silently, I cussed under my breath, because I did not have the time or patience for any bullshit today.

Larry looked over his shoulder. "Um, druid? I think you pissed 'em off."

"Ignore that, and finish your story."

"Ah, right. So Kiki hires this young, beautiful maid, drugs her, and tries to transfer her consciousness into the girl. Only problem is—"

"—Double D gave her the wrong incantations, or he transversed the symbology in the runes and wards."

The car roared toward us, screeching to a halt at the curb. The same mouthy fat kid who yelled at me pulled himself out of the window, poking his head and shoulders over the top of the cab. "Hey, fuckface, did you flip me off?"

I kept my eyes on Larry as I replied. "Yup. Here it is again, in case you missed it." I shot him the bird before addressing Larry. "Hang on a sec."

"Oh, this ought to be good," Larry muttered under his breath.

Car doors slammed as half a dozen college-aged jocks

climbed out of the vehicle, a late-model Mercedes AMG C-class. Nice car, actually—we'd salvaged one for parts a while back, and as I recalled it was pretty swank. I turned to face the lot of them as the loudmouth stalked around the car toward me, pushing his sleeves up.

"You think you're funny, don'cha, hipster?" he asked as he got up in my face.

The guy was about six-foot-three—a bit taller than me —and built like a defensive lineman. It was a good bet he'd spent most of his high school and college years throwing his weight around and intimidating the people around him. Guys like that were all blow and no go, in my experience. Sure, I could beat him down, but it'd be better to humiliate him in front of his friends. The lesson would last longer that way.

"Listen, slick—if you don't mind, I'd like to get back to having an in-depth discussion with my dog on the perils of necromancy," I said as I turned to face him. "So, if you're going to take a swing, hurry it up. I don't have all day."

"The perils of necro-what?" The guy's face broke into a haughty grin as he turned to look at his friends. "Can you believe this guy? What a fucking nutjob."

"He's just being a smartass, Owen. Teach him a lesson so we can get out of here already. Those girls from Zeta house aren't going to wait forever."

"Fuck it," Owen said as he clenched his fists.

I saw the punch coming from a mile away, especially since he telegraphed it by scrunching his face into a sneering grimace. Even without my Fomorian reactions, it looked like he was moving in slow motion as he pivoted behind the punch. With time to spare, I side-stepped and bitch-slapped him faster than he could react, but not so fast that he wouldn't know what happened.

My hand landed with a smack that echoed off the buildings across the street. Owen stumbled, both from the force of the slap and because he'd expected to make contact with that wide haymaker he'd thrown at me. I stood to the side as he recovered, hands behind my back as I whistled softly.

"Ooh, that looks like it hurt," I said in a low, calm voice. "Maybe you'd better go and drink that off, yeah?"

Owen's face turned red as he looked at me with incredulity, and then at his friends. Not quite as red as the handprint on the right side of his face, but still. Between the stunned looks on his friend's faces and the fact that his fists were balling up, I knew he'd take another swing. So, I smacked him again—lighter this time, but hard enough to sting.

Then, I smacked him again and again, until his facial expression transitioned from abject anger to utter confusion, and he was forced to raise his hands in a vain attempt to fend me off.

"Owen—it is Owen, right?" *Smack*! "Listen to me very carefully." *Smack*! "While this won't sink through your thick skull immediately, you're learning a valuable lesson today." *Smack, smack*! "That lesson is, there always someone out there who is bigger, stronger, and tougher than you." *Smack*! "Frankly speaking, you're damned lucky you learned that truth from a guy like me, rather than some random violent sociopath who'd sooner kill you than spit on you."

Owen dropped to the ground, and that's when I stopped hitting him. He curled up in a ball on the curb, hands covering his head as he cried crocodile tears. His friends stood aside, dumbstruck, although I counted it as sheer luck that they didn't have the balls to come to their buddy's rescue. Once I was certain they weren't going to jump in, I squatted next to their friend, balancing on the balls of my feet.

"Listen to me carefully," I said, reaching for him slowly. He flinched and cowered, and for a moment I felt really, really shitty. But only for a moment. "Relax—I'm not going to hit you anymore. But I want you and your gaggle of rich, entitled friends to get back in your car, stop harassing random people, and never darken this side of town again. You feel me, Owen?"

Snot ran down his face as he nodded, lip quivering.

"Good." I gently patted him on the cheek, like a parent comforting a child. "Glad we could have this talk."

Larry remained silent as Owen as his buddies quietly piled into the Mercedes. Once he started the car, the driver pulled a U-turn and they drove off, staying well under the speed limit.

"Holy cripes, druid. In all my life, I have never seen anybody break someone's spirit so ruthlessly and efficiently."

"Larry, I have zero time and even less patience for bull-shit like that right now. I'm running on almost no sleep, I have at least one and probably several gods hunting me, and I have less than 72 hours to stop an undead corgi necromancer from spreading the Z-vyrus in my city." I shrugged. "Besides that, I fucking hate bullies."

"I'd never have guessed," Larry replied. He cocked his head, ears twitching. "Say, you hear that?

31

I might not have had enhanced hearing in my human form, but even I could hear the weird drumming sound in the distance. I shaded my eyes with my hand, straining to see what it might be, but the source of the sound remained hidden over the rise in the distance. Yet it was getting louder—and closer.

Rattling off the words to a hearing enhancement cantrip, I cocked my head to focus in on the sound. There were two distinct rhythms, that much was plain, although I couldn't identify them. One was deeper and louder, like a bass drum being played in quick-time. The other sounded more like a snare drum, similar to the opening drum solo from an old Van Halen song my dad had liked.

Could it be... footsteps?

"You're hearing that, right, druid?" Larry asked.

"Yeah, I hear it." I reached for my Craneskin Bag—and promptly realized I'd left it inside the Druid Grove. "Shit.

Larry, run back to the junkyard and find Finnegas. Tell him to bring my Bag."

"You sure you don't need my help?"

"Now, Larry!"

"Okay, I'm goin', I'm goin' already."

The cryptid took off like a shot. I paid him no mind, instead searching the immediate environment for a suitable weapon. My eyes settled on a roughly three-foot-long piece of rebar sticking out of a pile of construction rubble just off the side of the road. It wasn't a sword, but it'd have to do. I jogged to the pile and pulled it out, finding it to be slightly longer than I thought, but serviceable just the same.

By that time, the clattering, clacking footsteps sounded as if they were almost upon me. Weapon in hand, I swung it experimentally a few times, then I turned to face the oncoming threat. As the source of the noise crested the hill, I blinked and rubbed my eyes to make sure I wasn't seeing things.

"What in the actual fuck is that?"

Larry chimed in beside me, slightly out of breath. "The one on the left looks like *Canis dirus*, otherwise known as the North American dire wolf. Or, at least, the skeleton of one."

"Okay, so I'm not imagining things. And the one on the right?"

"Saber-toothed. *Smilodon fatalis,* from the looks of it." He squinted his eyes, pausing for a moment. "Nope, I take that back. It's *Homotherium*, for sure—a scimitar-toothed cat."

"How do you...? You know what, never mind."

"You mean how do I know about Pleistocene-era megafauna? Those fuckers on Plum Island, that's how. Government scientists were obsessed with cloning saber-toothed tigers and short-faced bears from fossil DNA."

"I'd ask if they succeeded, but I don't think I want to know." Turning my attention to the threat at hand, I slammed the rebar into my palm as I watched the two massive animated skeletons bear down on us. "Fucking bone golems. This has to be Kiki's work."

"No doubt. This is exactly the type of nutty shit she'd come up with every time we had a fight. Do you know that one time she raised a mastodon out of the La Brea Tar Pits just because I forgot our anniversary?"

"Larry..."

"And the crazy thing was, it was mostly intact. Still had its sense of smell, and uncanny hearing, too. Chased me around for days, tracking me by scent and sound, until the damned spell wore off."

"Larry, I don't think this is the time—"

"Those were the days. Man, sometimes I miss that crazy bitch."

I decided to let him drone on, knowing from experience that he'd disappear long before he was in any real danger. Besides, the dire wolf and the saber-toothed tiger were nearly on top of us. Both had closed to within fifty yards, and they were hauling ass right at me. And hell if they didn't look hungry, if it were possible for a skeleton.

It had been a long time since I'd had to face real danger without my Fomorian powers. My stomach felt like it was full of butterflies, my legs trembled, and bile had risen to the back of my throat. My hands tightened on the rusted length of rebar, and I wished like hell I had Dyrnwyn in my hands.

"Ah, fuck it," I said, yelling over my shoulder as I took off at a sprint for the dire wolf. "Larry, go get my Bag from Finnegas."

"Again? I was just over there—"

"Would you go, already?"

Mid-stride I switched grips on the rebar, hefting it over my shoulder like a hunting spear as I muttered a spell. When I got within fifteen feet of the thing, I threw the length of iron with everything I had in me. After I launched the rebar, three things happened at once.

First, the makeshift spear sailed across the space between us, burying itself in the wolf's empty eye socket.

Second, the dire wolf kept coming without missing a single step.

And third, the saber-toothed cat leapt into an attack.

Well, fuck.

Rather than getting pounced on by the big cat or being bowled over and mauled by its companion, I dropped and slid at the wolf. As the cat sailed over me, the canid tried pulling up short, but it had too much momentum to stop quickly—especially since its bony paws didn't give it much traction on the asphalt. The great beast snapped its jaws at me as I slid under it, missing my nose by mere millimeters.

As I came out from under the wolf skeleton, I kicked its rear leg at the knee, buckling it. That caused it to stumble, which gave me just enough time to scramble to my feet before it turned on me. No way was I giving it a chance to recover. When the thing swung its head around, I shouted the trigger word to release my spell.

"*Liathróid dóiteáin!*"

A fireball roughly the size of a large watermelon exploded from my hands, enveloping the wolf's skull in yellow and blue fire. Bone, being mostly made up of minerals like calcium and phosphorus, was just about impossible to burn. But I knew from experience that intense heat could make it quite brittle, so I'd cranked up the intensity of the spell when I cast it.

Even at the hottest temperatures I could manage, that spell would take a minute to do its work. Thankfully the fire was distracting the bone golem, causing it to swing its head back and forth as it thrashed about in an attempt to extinguish the flames. While the dire wolf was preoccupied, I spun to face the cat as it circled around the wolf in an attempt to flank me.

32

There I was, facing down what was in essence a reanimated lion's skeleton, barehanded and without having prepared a second spell to deal with it. The good news was that an animal's skeleton only made up a small percentage of its total body mass, less than ten percent even in animals with the densest bone structure. So, I had a slight size and even bigger mass advantage working for me—but I was still fighting the animal version of the Terminator.

Part of my druid hunter training had been studying how various supernatural creatures attacked. The closest thing to the golem I could think of was a *cat sidhe*, a faery cat. That species preferred to sneak up on their prey and quickly snap their victim's neck with their powerful jaws. But when forced to attack from the front, they tended to latch on and disembowel their prey with their hind claws, much like any large cat would.

So, my only chance would be to grapple with the bone

golem, getting up close where the cat couldn't use its limbs and jaws to attack. And to hope like hell that the dire wolf would remain occupied as I did so. Then, if I could get in close enough to wrestle it, and if the dire wolf didn't recover and jump in the fray, maybe, just maybe, I could figure out a way to eliminate them both.

Easy, peasy. Right.

Unsure how to close the fighting distance with the great cat, the creature made the decision for me by leaping into another attack. With a battle yell that probably sounded more like a scared screech, I grabbed the cat's forelegs, rolling backward and pulling it over me with a weak *tomoe nage*, or circular throw. However, instead of kicking the skeleton over me I rolled over with it, simultaneously locking my legs around its torso and swimming inside its forelegs to hug it around the neck.

Then I held on for dear life. At first, the bone golem tried to scratch and bite me, to no avail. On discovering that it couldn't bring its most powerful weapons to bear, the big cat bucked, rolled, thrashed, and generally did everything possible to try to dislodge me. That turned out to be a mistake, because it allowed me to squirm to its back, much like a jiu-jitsu player going for the rear naked choke—a move that's a lot more brutal and not quite as pornographic as it sounds.

Once there, I had a brief moment of respite while the cat puzzled out what to do. In that moment, I caught a quick glance at the dire wolf, noting that the residual flames from my fireball spell were burning out. If that wasn't bad enough, the cat decided to roll to its feet and take off at a run toward the junkyard fence.

What the—? Oh, fuck me sideways.

Instead of leaping the fence and being fried by my wards, the damned thing ran parallel to the barrier, dragging me against it. Since the fence was made of corrugated sheet metal panels supported by thick steel pipe, it felt very much like I was being dragged across a giant cheese grater at speed.

"Ow, ow, ow, ow," I said every time I bounced off the fence. Soon I found my grip loosening, and I realized things were about to turn out very poorly for me if I didn't figure out a way to end this cat.

If only I could find a way to make it cross my wards. They'd negate the necromantic spell and de-animate this fucking thing.

Then it occurred to me—I was looking at the problem from the wrong angle. Actually, I didn't need to get it to pass my wards. Instead, all I had to do was apply the same de-animation magic to this creature's skeleton.

Clinging as tightly as possible to avoid being dislodged from the cat's back, I looked at the skeleton in the magical spectrum. Maintaining the concentration to do so while being dragged against a corrugated metal fence at 20 mph was a challenge, but it was that or be mauled to death by the animal versions of Jack Skellington. Despite the distractions, I soon detected the dark, sinuous weaves of magic that constituted Kiki's necromantic working.

From there, it was simply a matter of infusing those weaves with nature magic—in essence, life itself—to counteract the spell. By enforcing the natural order on the skeleton, my druid magic instantly negated Kiki's casting. As soon as it did, the bone golem collapsed in a heap below me—and I went tumbling into a nearby ditch.

Groaning loudly, I sat up, rubbing my shoulder and immediately regretting it. That whole side of my body was going to be one huge bruise tomorrow. I looked around to try to get my bearings, wondering where the dire wolf had gone. I doubted I could pull the same trick twice, as it'd be a hell of a feat to jump on the wolf's back in my current condition.

"Druid, look out!"

Larry's voice alerted me to the other bone golem's galloping approach, just in time for me to stumble to my feet and face it. Its skull was charred and blackened, and small wisps of flame and smoke curled in trails behind it as it ran at me. I noticed that the length of rebar was still stuck in its eye socket, and that gave me an idea.

This is going to hurt.

As the wolf lunged at me, I sidestepped and grabbed the iron bar with both hands, hearing the sizzle of my skin before I felt the burn. Ignoring the pain, I set my feet and pivoted as if I were a train conductor throwing a brake switch. My efforts were met by a satisfying *crack* as the skeleton's head split down the middle.

I held on to the rebar, despite the fact that it was so hot it was frying my hands. Yanking it free, I flipped it over, pulling seared skin and flesh from my palms and fingers as I did. Then I turned and brought it down on the wolf's head, shattering it to pieces. Instantly, the bone golem collapsed, much as its companion had moments earlier.

I discarded the still-smoking iron bar and sank to my knees, cradling my ruined hands against my torso. Seconds later, Larry shimmered into view a few feet in front of me with my Craneskin Bag in his mouth. He spat it out at my feet then sat back on his haunches, cocking his head as he looked me up and down.

"You know what, druid? You don't look so good. By the way, the old man found your Bag."

33

Minutes later, I sat in the junkyard office as Maureen fussed over my ruined hands and Finnegas worked on healing them. The old druid had gotten rid of the evidence, turning the now de-animated skeletons to ash before the cops arrived. Then, we'd beat feet back to the junkyard to avoid being questioned. I only hoped that no one had gotten video of the bone golems traipsing across South Austin—but if they had, I'd leave it to Maeve's fixers to sort that out.

Although my hands were a mess, I'd forgone a trip to the Grove to heal, because I wasn't about to let Larry out of my sight. And there was no way was I going to try to sneak him in, not after the manner in which the Grove had reacted to him earlier. As the old man spread dark-green goop on my burns, I glanced up to address both him and Maureen.

"You know, I could just shift real quick and—"

"No!" Finnegas and Maureen yelled in unison.

"Alright, sheesh."

Maureen glowered at Larry, who sat in the corner gnawing on a rawhide bone he'd found somewhere. That was one of the reasons why Roscoe and Rufus hated him so much—Larry was always stealing their stuff. Finding the chupacabra to be unimpressed with her glare, the half-kelpie turned it on me as she gave me my marching orders.

"There will be no shiftin' and bleedin' out, not if I have any say in the matter. Yer gonna sit right there and let the Seer heal ya', and that's that."

"But the deadline, and Kiki—"

"Nope, not gonna hear a word of it. Can't cast spells or swing a sword like that anyway. Naw, yer ta' park yer tail and wait 'til those burns heal. Then ya' can go gallivanting all over town chasing zombie pups ta' yer heart's content."

"Fine. Question is, what are we going to do about her?"

Larry stopped gnawing on his rawhide for a second to answer my question. "Aw, don't worry about it. Help is on the way."

"Somehow, I don't think I like the sound of that," Finnegas said, keeping his eyes on his task as he wrapped my hands in gauze.

"Hang on—just what do you mean by 'help'?" I asked. "Or rather, who?"

The chupacabra attacked the rawhide treat with gusto, growling as if it might surrender in fear at any moment. Then, he gave a creepy little dog shrug. "Just getting the old gang together. Same bunch of guys that helped me ditch her last time. Some pals from the old days."

"Now I'm sure I don't like it," Finnegas muttered as he tied the last knot on my bandages.

I started to rub my temples, cursing in frustration when I realized I couldn't. "Larry, when you say, 'the old days,' do you mean when you and Kiki met, or—?"

"Nah, that's recent history. I met these guys back on Plum Island. A couple of them helped bust me and the others out."

Finnegas stood up, reaching for his tobacco pouch. "This all sounds utterly disastrous, and I'll not hear another word of it. If anyone needs me, I'll be in the Grove taking a nap." As he was leaving, he gave me a withering look. "That's where you'd be, if you knew what was good for you. We may have two more days according to Maeve's clock, but Aenghus could show up any minute. The sooner we're ready to leave, the better."

"Yeah, I'm aware. But who's going to take care of this mess if I don't?"

Maureen shook her head. "Let the factions handle it. Eventually one of 'em will decide they don't want to take the heat. Then, they'll deal with it. No sense in you gettin' sidetracked cleaning up that mangy mutt's messes, not with Aenghus the Young breathing down yer' neck."

"Fine," I muttered. "But there's no way I'm taking my eyes off Larry, not with Kiki on the prowl."

Maureen rolled her eyes. "Suit yerself, but the mangy mutt managed ta' survive long before he met ya', and it's safe ta' say he'll do so long after yer' gone. Now, I have an appointment at the spa, so I'll leave ya' pair o' knuckle-heads to it."

After Maureen left, Larry continued to gnaw on the rawhide treat in silence while I surfed a few parts websites, looking for a new carb and headers for the Gremlin. An hour later, the chupacabra cleared his throat.

"Yes, Larry?"

"So, I was wonderin' if you had a plan for catching Kiki."

I kept my eyes on the screen, letting him stew for a few moments before I answered. "I've been thinking about it, yeah. But it's going to take more than me and you to pull it off, and I don't think Maureen and Finnegas are about to volunteer their help."

"Phew! That's a relief."

Swiveling my chair to face him, I snorted a derisive laugh. "A relief that we're short-handed, and we might not be able to pull off my plan?"

Larry's wheezing chuckle made him sound a bit like Dick Dastardly's sidekick, Muttley. "Aw, don't you worry about that. So long as you got a plan, we'll have plenty of hands to help."

I exhaled heavily, turning my eyes back to the screen. "Why do I have the feeling I'm going to regret getting involved in this mess?"

34

I spent the rest of the afternoon letting my hands heal while I prepared for nightfall, when I suspected that Kiki would return for round three. I'd already sent Roscoe and Rufus to the Grove for safekeeping and I'd sent the staff home early, so we had the junkyard to ourselves. Dusk had arrived by the time I'd nearly finished. I only hoped the precautions I'd taken would be enough.

As I finalized my preparations, Larry followed me around in silence, nodding and making inane, mostly supportive comments as I worked. "So, ya' think this is gonna work?"

"It'll have to, or else Austin is going to be overrun with zombie wildlife pretty damned quick. But if your friends don't show up soon, we're screwed, because I don't think we can spring this trap effectively ourselves. Now, if I could shift—"

"—you'd just tear through her minions and rip the

bitch's head off. You've said that a half-dozen times already."

I eyed the alterations I'd made to my wards and shrugged. "Yeah, well—I don't like how I nearly got my ass handed to me earlier by a couple of fossils."

"Like I said, I got some muscle coming. So, relax. All you gotta do is handle the magic side of things. I got the rest covered." Larry cocked an ear. "Speaking of which, I think I hear them coming now."

I couldn't hear anything at first, then I detected a familiar, yet somewhat disturbing, noise. It was the whooshing sound of a huge pair of leathery wings beating in the distance. As it grew closer, I started to get nervous. The last time I'd heard that sound was when I'd dealt with Camazotz, and I'd nearly been killed by a 3,000-year-old nosferatu the time before that.

"Larry—" I warned as my eyes scanned the dark, cloudy skies overhead.

"Sshh. Quiet, or you'll spook him. He's shy like that."

"Who's shy?"

Suddenly, the gibbous moon above was blocked out by a massive dark shape. I flinched involuntarily, then remembered that my wards would keep anything out of the junkyard that I didn't want to enter. But when that dark shape swooped down to land atop the peaked roof of the warehouse, I practically shit my pants.

I'd already started muttering the words to my fireball spell when Larry placed a paw on my foot. "Ixnay on the ell-spay, uid-dray. You wanna scare him off? Give him a moment to get used to us while we wait for the others to arrive."

It took a herculean effort of self-control to not attack this creature who'd so easily invaded my sanctum, because every cell in my body was screaming at me to blast it into the aether. Instead, I quickly cast a cantrip to enhance my senses so I could get a good look at it. As my eyes adjusted to the advancing dark, I took in every detail of the strange-looking beast on my warehouse roof.

The creature was tall, at least seven feet from head to toe, muscular, and humanoid in appearance, with a powerful build, rubbery gray skin, and clawed, webbed hands and feet. If I had to describe it in a word, I'd have called it demon-like, or perhaps gargoyle-like, although it was dissimilar enough to those species to indicate it was neither.

Of all its bizarre features, the thing's face and eyes were the most bothersome. For some reason, I couldn't seem to focus my eyes on its face. When I tried, all I saw was a large black blur. Even though I couldn't make out its facial features, its large, saucer-sized eyes shone bright red in the night, two glowing orbs that seemed to hypnotize me and draw me into their gaze.

I watched for several moments longer, mesmerized. Then it snapped its wings wide, folding them around its body as it crouched and settled into stillness.

"Druid. Druid. Drew-it!"

"Huh—what?" I said, shaking off the creature's spell. "What just happened?"

Larry clucked his tongue. "You can't stare at his eyes, or

else you'll get hypnotized. He can't help it, that's just the way they made him. Moe's actually kinda self-conscious about it, so if you can avoid it, don't do that again."

"Trust me, I won't." I rubbed my eyes, waiting for the strange stoned feeling to pass. "Mind telling me how 'Moe' bypassed my wards?"

"Same way I do. I'm a cryptid, right? Well, so's Moe. Sure, we got some supernatural DNA, a little alien DNA, and other stuff the mad scientists back at the lab threw in, but it's all mixed up and not enough to trigger your defenses."

I blinked and rubbed my head. "Ah, gotcha. Wait a minute, did you say 'alien DNA'? Because I distinctly thought I heard you say something about aliens."

"Did I say that? Hmm, that's weird. Hey, I think the other guys are here."

At that, Larry sped off like a bullet for the front gate. I took one last look at the dark figure above me, wondering what the hell it was. Then, it spoke. Not audibly, but directly into my brain.

-*Say, is there a bathroom around here?*- a sibilant, hissing voice said inside my head. -*We got tacos at this Mexican dive just outside of Houston, and now my stomach is a wreck.*-

I rubbed a gauze-covered hand across my face.

Ah, what the hell.

"Sure, through the door below you, down the hall, and to the right. If you go through the unmarked door right next to it, that's my old room. There's bottled water and Cokes in the mini-fridge, and coffee for the espresso machine. Help yourself."

The creature failed to respond, so a moment later I followed after Larry, turning my back on it against my better judgment. I was almost to the front office when I heard those massive, leathery wings unfurl with a snap, and it was all I could do to resist spinning to face it in a defensive crouch. As I slipped through the gate, I snuck a glance over my shoulder just in time to see a dark shadow slip silently into the warehouse.

Fucking hell, but my life is weird.

35

W hen I exited the front gate into the parking lot, an old, beat-up motorhome was pulling in front of the office. The damned thing was a dead ringer for Cousin Eddie's jalopy, the one from National Lampoon's *Christmas Vacation*. In fact, I half-expected Randy Quaid to jump out in boots and a bathrobe and loudly proclaim, "Shitter's full!" at any moment.

As the RV came to a stop, Larry bounced up and down with his tongue hanging out, wagging his tail furiously all the while.

"They're here, they're here," he squeed. "Druid, the gang's all here!"

"Great," I said under my breath.

Curious as to who—or what—might be behind the wheel, I tried my best to identify the driver through the windshield. But all I saw was someone in an oversized gray hoodie wearing dark sunglasses and a hospital mask. The driver must've noticed me looking, because he—or she—

gave me a sort of half-wave, half-salute before they ducked back into the RV's interior.

"Oh, man, has it been a long time since I saw these guys," Larry said. He'd stopped jumping around, but his little rat tail was still swinging a mile a minute. "You're gonna love these guys, druid. Salt of the earth is what they are, salt of the earth. Just don't play cards with Vinny. He don't like ta' lose, and he's been known to rip a guy's arm off once or twice."

"I'll keep that in mind," I said, sucking air between my teeth.

At that moment the door swung open, and a voice with a strong Jersey accent spoke from the dark interior. "Izza' coast clear?"

Larry gave another of his wheezing laughs. "C'mon, Dez, this is me you're talking to. Would I let my best friend get caught by those fuckers at Cerberus? Besides, this is Austin. People see weird shit here—they just think it's a shroom flashback or sumthin'."

Another voice echoed from the RV, a deep baritone that reminded me of Michael Clarke Duncan. "Hey, if Larry says it's cool, it's cool. Grab your shit and move, Dez, cuz' I gotta take a leak."

"Okay, I'm goin', I'm goin'."

When Dez—or rather, the one I assumed to be Dez—hopped out of the vehicle, my jaw hit the ground.

He was roughly five feet tall, with a kangaroo's lower body and hind legs, but with cloven feet like a goat and a thin, forked tail. His torso was more ruminant-like, but with leathery bat-like wings, stubby little T-rex arms that ended in clawed hands, and a head that was a cross between a goat and miniature pony. To top off his genetic-experiment-gone-horribly-wrong look, velvety, reddish-brown fur covered him from head to toe, and he had two short, pointed horns on his head that gave him a decidedly evil look.

That's the fucking Jersey Devil. Dez is the Jersey-fucking-Devil.

The cryptid clenched his cigar between his horse teeth, switching his can of Bud Light to his left as he extended a clawed hand toward me. "Desmond Cross, but you can call me Dez—everybody else does. Pleased ta' meet'cha, druid. Heard a lot about you."

To my credit, I only stared at his hand a moment before shaking it. "Colin McCool, welcome. I—haven't heard much about you, but I know Larry has been looking forward to your arrival."

I released Dez's hand, and he turned to give Larry a fake punch across the jaw. "This fuckin' Benny? He's probably already turned out your pockets for the debt he owes Vinny."

At that, Larry jumped and put his paws on Dez's chest and began licking his face. Dez pushed him away, laughingly.

"Alright already, I'm happy ta' see you too." Once Larry had settled down, Dez looked back inside the RV. "Hey, Vinny, you comin' or what?"

"Coming to whip your ass if you don't stop talkin' to me like I'm five," the deep voice boomed.

A second later a tall, hulking figure appeared in the

bus doorway. He wore a hoodie over a black t-shirt, dark sunglasses, a hospital mask, white jeans, and the biggest pair of Nike Airs I have ever seen. Now that I was up close, I could just make out the pebbly, scaly texture of his skin, expertly hidden under thick, flesh-colored makeup.

I had a pretty good idea what Vinny was, but I wasn't going to let him know I knew unless he chose to reveal his identity. So, I put on my best poker face and pretended I didn't see anything out of the ordinary—no small feat considering I was standing next to a chupacabra and the Jersey Devil. Stooping to exit the vehicle, the huge cryptid stood to his full height as he cleared the doorway, a full head-and-a-half taller than my 73 inches. Free from the confines of the RV, the fourth member of Larry's squad stretched his back with a loud groan, then he looked at me and nodded.

"Thanks for helping Larry out," he rumbled. "Not many folks would go out of their way to help someone like that. Especially not for one of us freaks, never mind going up against a crazy, dangerous bitch like Kiki."

Whether I wanted to admit it or not, I was getting comfortable with the idea that Larry's friends were all urban legends come to life. Maybe it was the fact that, despite how weird they looked, they spoke and acted like normal people. All except for Moe, that is. That fucker creeped me out.

"Don't mention it. By the way, the bathroom is in the big building to your left when you go through the gate. But fair warning, I think Moe got to it first."

Vinny hissed. "Son of a bitch—he's gonna stink the

place up, and nobody'll be able to go in there for a week. Told him not to order the *tripas* tacos, but the stupid fucker never listens."

I covered my mouth to hide a smile. "There are some port-a-potties out in the junkyard. I can't vouch for how sanitary they are, though."

"Gonna have to powder your face later, Vin," Dez said as he pointed his cigar at the sky to the north. "Looks like the Queen Bitch of Crazy is about to make her entrance."

36

Dez must've had much better eyesight than mine, because I couldn't make out a thing in the night sky except for clouds and the moon above. However, my plan depended on us being safely ensconced inside my wards, before Kiki attacked. Visible threat or no, we needed to be inside the junkyard before she arrived.

"C'mon, everyone—let's head inside and I'll fill you in on the plan," I said, trying to avoid sounding bossy as I did so.

Vinny chuckled as he addressed the chupacabra standing in front of him. "You hear that, Larry? The kid has a plan. How refreshing."

"Hey, I had a plan the last time, didn't I?" Larry replied. "How was I supposed ta' know we set up our ambush on a Native American burial ground?"

Dez scratched his upper lip with a claw, snickering. "Coulda' been the burial mound you picked out 'cause it was 'high ground'—just shootin' in the dark here."

While they razzed Larry, I kept my eyes on the sky. Soon, my magically-enhanced vision allowed me to pick out a tiny dot flying over downtown Austin and moving quickly in our direction. As the object grew closer, its shape became more distinct—and disturbing. It appeared to have a long torso, two heads, and huge wings, with one head being misshapen and elongated, and the other small and round.

What the hell is that?

"Fellas, I don't know what that thing is, but it's moving fast," I said nervously. "Maybe we should get inside."

The trio ignored me, instead remaining focused on the discussion at hand. Namely, how Larry had almost gotten them killed the last time they'd faced Kiki.

"Next time you can plan the ambush!" Larry said loudly.

"Maybe I will!" Vinny replied.

"Just like you planned this trip?" Dez asked, looking askance at Vinny. "You booked us a camping spot at an RV park in Honobia. Frickin' Honobia, home of Oklahoma's largest annual Bigfoot festival! We hadn't even finished setting up camp when those wannabe cryptozoologists came sniffing around. If it hadn't been for Moe hypnotizing them, we'd all be on the front page of next week's *National Enquirer*."

By that point Kiki was almost upon us, and as it so happened, she wasn't flying a two-headed bird. Somehow, she'd managed to find a mostly-intact pterosaur carcass, reanimating it to serve as her ride. The thing was huge, with a 40-foot wingspan, teeth like daggers, and claws like railroad spikes. When it saw us, the creature's cry pierced the night, sounding like a cross between the roar of a lion and a woman's scream.

And even that failed to get the cryptids' attention.

As Larry and his friends argued, the zombie corgi necromancer sat astride the pterosaur's back like a valkyrie riding into battle, barking up a storm with a maniacal look in her glowing green eyes. Incongruously, she had a pretty pink bow tied in a top-knot between her ears, and she wore a pink and gray turtleneck dog sweater that matched her bow perfectly. For an undead animal, I noted that she was remarkably well-preserved. And agile as well, riding the pterosaur like a surfboard as it quickly banked and dove straight at us.

"Guys," I warned, "you might want to duck."

I hit the deck, Larry slipped under a car, and Dez simply took a knee. Their scaly pal, on the other hand, ripped off his mask, sunglasses, and hoodie, revealing exactly what I'd suspected,

Vinny was a lizardman.

"Hah—I knew it," I said to no one in particular.

Vinny looked like a darker, greener version of Killer Croc in the original *Suicide Squad* movie. Personally, I'd thought it was a shitty depiction of the super-villain, and that the *Arkham Origins* Croc was the best animated version of the character. However, proportion-wise, Vinny filled the role nicely—and honestly, he could've stood in for the creature on film and no one would've been the wiser.

Dez gave me a withering look. "Oh really, Sherlock?

What gave it away, his silky-smooth complexion, or the mouth full of needle-sharp teeth?"

As the pterosaur and the diminutive canine necromancer nose-dived right at him, Vinny calmly tossed his sunglasses to Dez.

"Hold these, will you?" he asked, squaring his shoulders and looking straight up at the plummeting mass of zombified reptile and dog.

Dez gave me a horse's grin. "Watch this, kid."

"I can't look," Larry said, covering his eyes with his paws.

"I can't look away," I said, spellbound by the spectacle unfolding right before my eyes.

The pterosaur spread its massive jaws wide, clearly aiming to cut Vinny in two as it crashed into the lizardman. But at the last second the tall, heavily-muscled cryptid crouched and sprang to his left, raking the giant flying reptile's wing as he did. Then he leapt atop a nearby car, well out of the pterosaur's reach, leaving the reptile's right wing in tatters.

Rather than staying out of the winged lizard's way, Vinny attacked, circling while darting in and out to swipe at its face, wings, and torso. Grounded now, the pterosaur was awkward and out of its depth on the ground. Although it could quickly dart out and snap at the lizardman with its beak, its opponent was that much faster, and clearly never in danger.

This all served to infuriate Kiki, who screamed obscenities at both Vinny and her flying lizard. "You stupid fucking piece of shit, good for nothing pterodactyl, what the hell did I bother raising you for if you can't even kill one measly mistake of science? And you, Vinny—I'm gonna turn you into a fucking set of luggage by the time this is done!"

Clearing my throat, I pointed at Vinny. "Um, do you think he needs help?"

"Nah, he's fine," Dez replied, giving a nod at the gate. "You got this fence warded, kid?"

"Does Iron Man wear a bulletproof codpiece? Of course I have it warded," I replied.

Dez gave the chupacabra a wink. "I'm startin' ta' like this punk, Larry."

Larry crawled out from his hiding spot. "Yeah, I suppose he's handy to have in a pinch. Ready to go see if Moe's done destroying Colin's bathroom?"

"Let's," Dez replied. "Then we can deal with Fatal Attraction over there, for good."

37

As we ducked through the gate, Dez leaned his head out to yell at his pal. "Yo, Vinn-ee! Finish that up, will ya?"

"Coming," the lizardman yelled in reply.

Meanwhile, the sounds of battle—and Kiki's non-stop cursing—raged on.

Dez shut the gate, latching it from the inside. "Okay, kid, what's your plan?"

"It's simple—we're going to let Kiki inside the junkyard."

The Jersey Devil pulled his cigar stub from his mouth, turning to face Larry with a look that said I was a dumb-shit. "Larry, I thought you said this kid was smart."

"I never said that," Larry replied. "I just said he knew how to kill necromancers. He iced Kiki's mentor, after all."

The little devil creature nodded, giving me an appraising look. "That was you, eh? Damned impressive, taking that fucker out."

"How'd you hear about it?" I asked, perplexed.

He chewed on his cigar stub and shrugged. "Being the outcasts of the supernatural world, we cryptids tend to stick together. La Onza's well-known among our kind, so..."

"Makes sense," I said.

Dez frowned and nodded. "Anyway, how're you gonna kill that bitch?"

"Oh, right," I answered, distracted yet again by the weirdness of it all. "I'm going to let her think that she's broken through my wards, then I'm going to light those puppies up and trap her in here."

"Ah, I get it," Larry said. "Then we lock the place up and throw away the key. Brilliant!"

"Um... no, Larry," I said. "This junkyard employs a lot of people, so I need to keep it operational. Besides, she'd break out eventually anyway."

"But we'd be long gone by then. I fail to see an issue with that plan."

Dez cracked his neck loudly. "Stop being a putz, Lar. Sheesh."

"Anyway, once we get her inside, we'll have the advantage. There's just one of her and four of us, plus I know this place like the back of my hand."

"Seems reasonable," Dez replied. "I like it."

"I still say we should lock her in here," Larry groused under his breath.

Just then, Vinny came sailing over the fence, landing hard enough in a pile of discarded tires to bury himself. Moments later, a green, scaled hand shot out of the pile.

"I'm fine, in case anyone wants to know. By the way, Kiki is flipping pissed, and she brought company."

"What's new?" Dez muttered. "Now, quit screwing around and go find Moe. Somethin' tells me we're going to need his creepy ass."

Vinny extricated himself from the pile of tires, walking toward the warehouse as he complained under his breath. "Oh, I see how it is. Y'all wanna make a lizardman do all the hard work. Shit ain't gonna be like this forever, ya' know. One day, this lizardman's gonna rise up, and..."

Larry, Dez and I stood in uncomfortable silence until Vinny's voice faded into the distance.

"He's still on that 'fight the power' kick?" Larry asked.

"It comes and goes," Dez replied. "Every once in a while, I'll point out that all cryptids are minorities, just to piss him off."

"He is kind of pulling more than his fair share of the weight," I proffered.

"Thank you!" Vinny shouted in the distance.

Dez hocked up a ball of phlegm and spat it out. "That's just because he's our starting pitcher. Trust me, once Kiki gets in here, things are going to go sideways and we'll all have to do our part."

There was a loud boom as the gate to the junkyard shook on its hinges, perfectly punctuating Dez' point. "Looks like it won't be long," I said, checking the weaknesses in my wards that I'd left as a decoy. "Let's get moving so we're not standing here when she rides that pterodactyl corpse into the yard."

As Kiki's attempts to breach the gate grew in ferocity,

we jogged past the warehouse toward the stacks. I had a few surprises planned for her there, not the least of which was the Druid Oak. It hated necromancy in all its forms, and I was sure it'd waste no time in helping me destroy the tiny necromancer and her pets.

I pulled up short in a clearing close to the Oak. Dez and Larry followed my lead, looking at me expectantly as Vinny came bounding up behind them.

Dez bit the tip off a fresh cigar, spitting it out before speaking. "Alright, kid—this is your turf, so it's your show. Whazza' plan?"

I glanced at Vinny. "Is Moe coming?"

"Yeah, he'll be here. He's still on the pot, but it sounded like he was finishing up. I didn't get close enough to find out for certain, though. It's like fucking Mogadishu in there. Lawd help anyone who needs to use those facilities for the next few days."

"Um, that's more information than I needed, but okay." I made eye contact with each cryptid in turn. "I've dealt with necromancers before, and you guys have too, so I don't need to tell you to watch your six. Necros love raising corpses behind their enemies, and the fucking dead'll creep up on you before you know it."

Larry nodded enthusiastically. "Don't have to tell me twice. Can't tell you how many times that crazy bitch snuck a stiff into our bed. I'd be slappin' them cheeks, and all of a sudden, bam, there's a fresh corpse trying to stick its finger up my ass. I—"

Dez slapped one of his small, clawed hands over

Larry's snout, clamping it shut. "Ya' done?" Larry nodded. "Please continue, druid."

"I'll have that image seared into my memory for all time, so thanks for that," Vinny muttered.

"You and me both," I said, squatting as I started making chicken scratches in the dirt. "Now, here's the plan. Vinny will draw Kiki and any of her heavy hitters into the yard over here. Dez and Larry will keep her distracted while I lock her in and work on permanently deleting everyone's favorite zombie corgi."

-*What about me?*- a creepy voice said in my head.

"Fuck, Moe!" Dez protested. "How many times I gotta' tell you not to do that? It's fuckin' rude, like an invasion of privacy or some shit."

"Sorry," the demonic nightmare creature said in a high, whiny voice reminiscent of Rick Moranis in *Ghostbusters*. "It's just easier, and you know I don't like the way my voice sounds."

"Don't sweat it—telepathy will come in handy in the coming fight," I said, even though I didn't mean it. "You're our air support. Stay close, kill anything that Kiki has in the air, and pull out anyone who gets in over their heads."

"I can do that," Moe said. "And sorry about your bathroom."

38

A t that, the gate gave way with a resounding crash, announcing Kiki's entrance. And if that wasn't enough to let us know she was coming, the crazy little weirdo magically enhanced her voice. It was as if someone had given a megaphone to Teresa Giudice after a long afternoon at the bar and a surprise guest appearance by Danielle Staub.

"Larry, you fucking low-life canine piece of shit, where are you? I'm gonna rip your tiny wrinkled balls off, shove them down your throat, and then pull 'em back up and make you eat 'em again! Nobody walks out on Kristina Katrina Esposito and locks her inside a Native American burial mound, you sorry excuse for a sixth husband —nobody!"

"Well, at least she avoids racially-sensitive language," I said as Dez and I ducked behind the rusted cadaver of a late 70s Monte Carlo.

"Oh, thank heavens for that," Dez replied with an eye

roll. "It's a huge comfort to know that she'll eschew the use of racial epithets and gender-normative pronouns as her undead army eats our intestines like spaghetti."

"Geez, dude, lighten up already," Larry's disembodied voice said from somewhere nearby. "The kid might be a bit of a hippy, but he's just trying to lighten the mood."

"Nobody says 'hippy' anymore, Larry," I replied. "And if you say 'hipster,' I'll kill you myself."

Dez busted out laughing. "See, now that's funny."

"Har, har," Larry said. "By the way, she's here."

I peeked over the car's hood just in time to see Kiki enter the clearing astride her now grounded pterosaur. Following in her wake was a menagerie of animals—all dead, reanimated, and in various states of disrepair. Most looked as though they'd been roadkill that the tiny necromancer had raised on her way over, but I strongly suspected that more than a few Austinites were missing their pets this evening.

I counted at least a half-dozen dead deer, a few dead hogs and armadillos, a slew of cats and dogs, and a bunch of squirrels, raccoons, rabbits, and skunks thrown in for good measure. Moreover, there were hundreds of dead bats and birds fluttering around above our heads. And to round things out, Kiki had raised several rattlesnakes that were taking up the rear.

Just when I thought it couldn't get weirder, a bull marched into the yard. From the looks of it, it was a full-grown male Santa Gertrudis, with a mature and unshorn set of horns, a missing eye, and a seriously nasty disposition. If I had to guess, I'd say it easily weighed two thousand pounds, give or take a few for various missing internal organs.

"Where the hell did she find a dead bull in the middle of Austin?" Dez asked.

"This is Texas," I replied. "She probably found it in someone's backyard."

About that time, Vinny leapt over a stack of cars, hooting at the top of his lungs as he landed on the bull's back. "Woo-hoo, I always wanted to be a cowboy!"

"Ride 'em, Vin!" Larry cheered, as Dez shook his head in embarrassment.

Immediately, the bull had a shit attack of the highest order, bucking and spinning and snorting in an attempt to get the lizardman off its back. Then, it was chaos. Dead animals scattered everywhere in an attempt to get out of the bull's way, several went flying upon being kicked by the bull's rear hooves, and even more were trampled underfoot.

This in turn spooked the pterosaur, who in its defense had probably never seen a lizardman ride a zombie bull before. That caused Kiki's undead steed to back up until it stepped on one of the Oak's roots. And that's when things really went haywire.

Instantly, the Oak sent me an image of a raging storm, followed by that of a mama bear defending her cubs, followed by a tornado plowing across the plains. In other words, the Oak was pissed, and it was about to go down. I said the trigger word to slam my wards back in place so none of the undead animals could escape. Then, I took off at a sprint for the back side of the yard.

As they say, no plan survives contact with the enemy.

"Run, everyone—the shit is about to hit the fan!"

"Don't need to tell me twice," Larry replied, his voice fading into the distance.

Dez, on the other hand, was living up to his reputation by putting his kangaroo legs to good use. He leapt from car to car, easily clearing thirty-foot gaps in a single leap. At first I thought he was running away from the fray. Then I realized he was stomping on random undead creatures with every leap, snapping necks and spines as he landed with those weird cloven feet.

"Well, that's something you don't see every day," I quipped before looking back to see how the lizardman was doing. He was still riding the bull like a rodeo cowboy going for the eight-count, although the first eight seconds had already passed. Cupping my hands, I yelled to warn him of the coming carnage. "Vinny, get out of there—shit's about to get real!"

"Aw, man, I was just getting the hang of this," he yelled as he did a backflip off the bull onto a nearby stack of cars. He stood there for a moment, looking for signs of danger while batting away the occasional flying zombie creature that tried to sink its teeth into his thick, scaled skin. He looked at me, his hands raised questioningly. "What's up, druid? I don't see no—"

That's when the ground erupted, all across the yard.

39

One moment, the ground was solid beneath Kiki's pterosaur and the dozens of animals she'd raised. The next, hundreds of roots, vines, and plants burst from the ground, wrapping around random animals like boa constrictors, breaking limbs, crushing ribs, and snapping necks with abandon. It was then I learned that even undead creatures could shriek in fear, as a few dozen zombified animals cried out all at once.

I felt sorry for them, really I did—but this was for the best. They had to be suffering and in pain, being raised from the dead half-decomposed and with horrible injuries. Besides, I knew from my time in the Hellpocalypse that they likely only still possessed the lowest of brain functions. Thus, they probably weren't even aware of what was going on, and their screams were merely an instinctive response to danger.

Knowing that still wouldn't get their screams out of my head, though.

I observed the carnage from atop a car's hood, picking off the odd undead animal that had managed to escape the Oak's fury with careful shots from my Glock. In the distance, the bull put up a hell of a fight, but in the end, dozens of thorny vines pulled it into a dusty, scrapyard grave beneath the Earth's surface. The pterosaur was about to suffer a similar fate from the looks of it, and Kiki grew even more livid as the great beast began to falter.

"Fuck you, you big freak of nature!" she shouted as she ran frantic circles around the pterosaur's back. "You think you can take Kiki Esposito off the board, but I got a surprise for ya', ya' oversized houseplant."

And at that Kiki turned around, lifting her tail and pointing her hind end at the vines shooting up from the ground around her mount. The zombie corgi barked, then a ball of sickly-green, phantasmic fire burst out of her ass at the vines. The virescent light enveloped the plant-life, and where it did, the vines and roots withered away.

"Did that crazy bitch just shit death magic out her ass?" Dez asked from across the yard.

"Huh. I was wondering how a creature with no hands cast spells," I observed. "Gross, but strangely practical, if you think about it."

"I can't believe you hit that," Vinny remarked drily from his perch atop a stack of cars to my right.

"Hey, it's not like she did that in bed," Larry said in his defense.

Clearly, Kiki's plan was to free her mount so she could make her escape. The flying lizard's wing was already being mended by eerie green wisps of energy, and Kiki's necromantic ass magic was doing a fine job of forcing the Oak to keep its distance. Soon, the corgi necromancer had cleared enough space for the pterosaur to take flight.

If they got airborne, it would pose a serious problem, considering that the anti-necromantic wards I'd cast only covered about fifty vertical feet from the ground. That was plenty high enough to keep any stray undead animals in as we cleaned them up, but Kiki's steed could clear that easily. The corgi released a few more balefire farts for good measure, then the pterodactyl flapped its wings and took off, rising in lazy circles that would soon take it up and over my wards.

"Druid, she's gettin' away!" Larry shouted.

"I can see that, Larry," I growled.

-Is it time for me to jump in?- Moe's creepy voice said in my head.

"Yes!" everyone said at once.

The only response we heard was a strange whistling noise that came from the skies above us. It rapidly grew in volume, changing from a high-pitched teakettle sound to the roar of a plummeting jetliner.

"What's that?" Kiki asked, a note of concern in her voice as her eyes scanned the skies overhead. Then, she broke out in laughter. "Seriously, you're relying on Moe to stop me? The only thing he's good for is crop-dusting parties and carpet-bombing bathroom stalls. Puh-leze."

"She's one to talk," Vinny said as he landed next to me.

"Is she right, though?" I asked. "Does Moe have this?"

"Oh, he's got it," Vinny replied with a sly, serpentine

grin. He crossed his arms and pointed his chin at the sky. "Watch."

"Hah, we're almost over your wards, druid. Ya' thought you were smarter than Kiki Esposito, but nobody's bested me yet. Not even that worthless piece of shit they call the Dark Druid. Or, as I refer to him, deadbeat husband number three. I told that rat bastard, if you leave me, I'm gonna haunt you to the ends of the Earth, but did he listen—?"

At that moment, a huge black and red missile impacted both Kiki and the pterosaur dead center, doing about 300 miles an hour. The impact pretty much disintegrated the pterosaur and zombie dog both, pelting us with a rather nasty downpour of undead lizard and dog parts. The stench was unreal, instantly filling the yard with a smell not unlike a five-day-old roadkill skunk in July.

Moe came to a pinpoint stop, hovering in the air ten feet above the center of the yard. "Did I do good?" he asked in his high, meek voice.

"Perfect," I said, wiping a piece of rotten pterodactyl guts from my face. I slung it off to the side, forcing a smile. "The Oak needed fertilizing anyway."

"Now, why didn't he do that the last time?" Vinny asked in an annoyed voice. "Coulda' saved us a hell of a lot of trouble, not to mention that the bitch wouldn't have come back for round two."

Moe shrugged. "I had six bowls of three-bean chili for lunch that day, so you guys ditched me at that trucker plaza in South Amboy. Took me all night to find you, and when I did, she was gone."

"Worth it not to smell that stench," Dez said, wiping unidentified goop from his brow. "Worse than this mess by a mile."

I glanced around, looking for the chupacabra who was the cause of the whole sordid affair. "Larry, you can come out now. She's gone."

"Oh, I know," he softly replied from somewhere nearby.

"Are you cryin'?" Vinny growled. "'Cause if you are, I'm gonna kick your skinny rat ass all the way back to Jersey."

"Yeah, he's cryin' alright," Dez remarked.

"It's just..." Larry replied with a hitch in his voice. I noted that he'd wisely chosen to stay invisible for the moment.

"Yes?" I asked, impatience creeping into my voice.

Larry sniffled loudly. "I just—I just wonder what that undead threesome woulda' been like, is all. Now I'll never know."

"I'm gonna kill him," Vinny said. "I swear it."

"Not if I get to him first," I hissed.

"I get the first swing," Dez said, slapping a fist into his open palm.

"Aw, c'mon now, guys," Larry said. I heard his claws scrambling to gain purchase on the roof of a nearby car. "Let's talk this out, rational-like and all—like pals."

"Nope," Dez said.

"Uh-uh," Vinny agreed.

"I could really go for some bean and cheese nachos and a cold Modelo right now," Moe opined.

"No!" everyone shouted in unison.

GET A FREE BOOK!

Visit my website at MDMassey.com to get a free copy of the ebook version of *Druid Blood*, a Colin McCool prequel novel. Once you're there, simply enter your email so I'll know where to send it!

Made in the USA
Monee, IL
18 March 2024

55209138R00114